DUNCAN PRYDE SERIES **2**

RAINE OF

TERROR

JAN DOMAGALA

THE
GL🌐
BAL
—— *EDIT*
The international imprint of REDFeather Penguin

Published by Red Penguin Books

Bellerose Village, New York

ISBN

Digital 978-1-63777-495-3

Print 978-1-63777-496-0

Contents

Prologue

Altair, 2287ce

Tamara Hitoshi had been the director of the bio genetics facility for just one year. In that time, she had increased productivity and instituted new safety protocols ensuring that the facility could not be infiltrated nor attacked from outside.

Today all that would be to no avail.

A product of the finest education money could buy, she had worked her way up through various companies until she found her way to her present position.

At thirty-three years old, she was one of the youngest people to reach such a prestigious position.

Sitting in her office going through the daily logs, she was alarmed by the sound that split the air. The computer suddenly began to broadcast the 'intruder alert' alarm throughout the entire facility.

Getting to her feet, she ran toward the door. In the corridor outside, people were running for cover as explosions rent the air and shook the walls. Smoke billowed down the length of the corridor as walls collapsed and dark clad armed figures dropped down through holes in the roof.

Bullets raked the wall and she ducked back inside her office, the fear gripping her almost paralysing her body.

Cowering down behind her desk, she heard the door burst open and a tall figure wearing a mask and carrying a deadly looking rifle walked over to her.

"Stand up Director, I need your access code to the Black Vault," he said.

"Why do you need that?" she asked, slowly getting to her feet, her curiosity momentarily overcoming her fear.

"Isn't that obvious Director? There is something in there I want, and I need you to get it for me," he replied.

"I can't do that," she said adamantly.

Grabbing her by the shoulder, he dragged her from around the desk and took her to the door. Continuing down the corridor, he dragged her with him to an open area where several people were lined up against a wall. Standing in front of them were the other dark clothed figures all aiming their rifles at them.

"You have a choice to make, Director. Give me what I want or these people all die. Not at once as that would prove futile. If I kill them all now, then I have no leverage over you. I understand that as well as you. You are an educated woman, so I'm sure you can guess how this will work. You refuse, I kill one person and then another until you see them all die, or you give me what I want," the figure said then he nodded to his men, who shot one of the people against the wall.

A burst of automatic rifle fire slammed the figure against the wall, blood dancing from each impact as the unlucky individual was killed.

"No!" she screamed futilely.

"That was to prove my sincerity and determination, Director. I never bluff, I never make a threat I cannot carry out. So, now you know where you stand in all of this. If you want to survive this little encounter and save the rest of these people's lives, I suggest to do as I ask."

Looking at all the terrified faces of the people who worked for her, she knew there was only one decision she could make.

"Okay, I'll give you what you want," she acquiesced, her head dropping to her chest in defeat.

The Black Vault was in the lowest level of the facility. The armed men took everyone down to it just to keep the pressure on Hitoshi. They lined the workers up against the back wall as they took the director to the vault. It wasn't like a bank vault but a door to a biosecurity zone. It was in this vault that biohazards were stored. It was the highest level of protection, classified P5. Centuries before, the highest level of protection was P4, but since space travel had been more prominent, a new level was needed for pathogens found on far off worlds.

Hitoshi stood in front of the vault door, which had a panel to the side. First, she placed her right hand over a palm reader. A blue strip light ran up then down the length reading her palm print, then she placed her right eye up to an ocular scanner. This read her retina pattern. Finally, she placed her right hand into a slot which jabbed a sharp needle into her finger to draw a drop of blood. In seconds, the blood was scanned and a DNA pattern was found and matched against hers, which was on record in the computer files. The three security measures put together were considered to be fool proof, one, maybe two of them could be duplicated but not the third as well.

The door opened to an airlock, which two of the men entered. Inside the airlock they stepped into biohazard suits then went through into the main vault room. In less than two minutes, they were emerging from the airlock carrying a case they had taken with them.

Hitoshi wondered what they had taken from the vault, as only the worst things imaginable were stored in there. Her fear spiked when she saw them come out and the door close behind them.

"All sorted Boss," one of them said to the man in charge.

"Make your way to the exfil," he said, and he gave another signal to his men.

They opened fire on the people lined up against the wall, their bullets shredding their torsos, ripping the life out of them. As they fell to the floor, blood stained the wall which they had stood in front of seconds earlier.

"You said you'd let them live," Hitoshi screamed at the man by her side. The horror she felt widened her eyes as she could guess what was coming next.

"I lied," the man said as he brought up a pistol to her head and fired. The bullet took out her forehead smashing through her brain killing her instantly.

If she had still been alive, she would have seen the black clad figures leave taking with them whatever it had been they had stolen from the vault. She never saw that though, the bullet that had killed her prevented all of that. It also prevented her from warning the galaxy of what had happened here. In a way, she had been spared the horror of what was to come, killing her had been a favour, one she could never be grateful for.

Chapter 1

Terra II

Duncan Pryde was enjoying himself. For the first time in months since the death of his parents, he had allowed himself time and room to escape and relax.

One of the things he and his father liked to do was climb. It had been his father who had first taken him on his first climbing trip. He had been in his early teens and looking for direction in his life. The discipline needed to climb a rock face helped to give him focus, and it was here that he first learned he could control his emotions in a way few others could.

Considered by some to be a psychopath, he was in reality more of a functioning sociopath in the respect that, unlike true sociopaths who had no empathy and a high tolerance towards fear, he had the same emotions that everyone else had. He felt fear, rage, love, he had empathy for others, but where sociopaths had none of these and had to mimic them, he could control his to the point of closing his mind off towards them. This was extremely helpful in his job as an operative of the Ministry of Intelligence. When needed, he would shut off all his emotions so he could perform more efficiently, unencumbered by fear or empathy toward his enemies he would act immediately without doubt to hinder him.

This was his first holiday for years, and he was enjoying it more than he thought he had reason to. He had visited one of the locations he and his father had visited in years gone by, and he had spent the last week or so pushing himself to the limit, climbing several rock faces. He was reaching the top of the face he had left until the last; it was the favourite of his dad's.

A vertical face of granite that stretched up to the heavens for over fifteen hundred metres. It was called Heaven's Gate because many climbers had fallen to their deaths attempting this climb and those who succeeded had always said they felt closer to heaven once they reached the summit.

He was within reach of the summit, just another few metres to go, but there was a particularly dangerous overhang to navigate first.

As he looked up, he could see the overhang. It reached out for at least half a metre, so he carefully made his way under it. Reaching over his head and leaning back away from the rock face, he managed to place his fingers over the top of the ledge. Moving up farther, he had to make a move then. The ledge awaited and to get over it, he would have to release his grip on the face. This was the most dangerous part of the manoeuvre. He had one hand on the ledge, one on the wall face and both feet ready to kick off.

Kicking off with both feet he swung off from the face then threw his other hand onto the ledge and heaved himself up. Pulling his entire body up with just the strength of his arms, he was able to throw a knee onto the ledge and then scramble over it. Once there, he could reach the summit in a few seconds.

The view from the top was breath-taking, and a smile crossed his rugged features as he looked out over the expanse of forest surrounding the base of this climb. Sweat glistened on his body in the sunlight from the clear sky overhead. He was content for the first time in a long time.

For the climb, he had worn a tee shirt and shorts with a pair of climbing shoes. Around his waist, he wore a belt with moisture absorbing powder in a pouch to help his grip and his Personal Information Network pad in another pouch. He never went anywhere without it; it was a prerequisite of his job as an operative.

As he was taking in the view, he heard a chime on his PIN which connected to his earbud. It told him a call was coming in.

"Duncan, C has instructed me to issue a recall on you. Something has come up and he needs to see you in his office right away," the voice said in his ear. It was a voice he recognised, the voice of Stephanie Goodchild who was the assistant to Chambers, his boss in MI7.

"Copy that, I'm on my way," he replied.

"I've sent a shuttle to you to bring you straight here. There's no time to wait for you to get down from that thing."

Just as she finished saying that, the sound of the shuttle's engines was heard approaching from above.

A ladder was dropped from the hatch in the side which he grabbed onto and was hauled up from the top of Heaven's Gate.

As soon as he was inside, the shuttle peeled away and sped off toward the city.

Work was calling and he found as soon as he got the call, he was ready to return to it.

Chapter 2

Mi7 Hq

Duncan Pryde arrived at the new headquarters for MI7 wearing a change of clothes that had been on the shuttle for him.

MI7 was the short form for Ministry for Intelligence section Seven, which was the department that dealt with Security Operations, or SecOps. The old base, Station Five, had been attacked a few months back by a faction of the Coalition Intelligence Agency, actually the Director who regarded MI7 to be barring his path and an enemy to the Coalition Of Planets. He had acted on his own, but it had illustrated a flaw in the structure of the organisation and President Harada had instructed that the CIA henceforth would be absorbed into the Ministry for Intelligence. In this way, there would be no more internecine struggles for power.

Director William Chambers was still in command of MI7, but his budget had been increased and a new headquarters allocated whilst the old HQ was dealt with.

Sitting on the edge of the river that ran through one of the largest cities on the planet, New London, the new HQ was hidden in plain sight. It had been deemed too dangerous to announce where it was or what it was, so they had chosen a travel business named Universal Travel as a front for their secretive work. UniTrav, as it was known, dealt with all forms of travel but concentrated on the high-end clients who could afford specialist treatment. To that end, the agents of MI7 could go anywhere under the pretext of ensuring each destination was up to their exacting standards. It nestled near the bank of the river, giving it access to it and the wonderful views of the city beyond.

The actual base was hidden beneath this business in tunnels excavated much earlier that gave access to the river and the landing pads used for the flights. No one would suspect if a boat left the scene or if a flight took off from one of the landing pads or runways. It was the perfect cover.

Pryde was taken through into the front entrance to one of the elevators that descended into the actual headquarters by one of the flight crew. Once he was in the elevator, he was left alone to find his way.

At the bottom, he left the elevator and followed the signs pointing the way to Chambers' office. Not having much of an idea where things were in this new headquarters, he was pleased to see a friendly face he knew would point him in the right direction.

"Duncan, you're looking well and rested. How was the climb?" Stephanie Goodchild said. She was slim and attractive with deep auburn hair that framed an open and friendly face that had eyes that twinkled with a mischievous smile all of their own.

Her usual attire of white blouse and pencil skirt was present and correct, showing she was ready for work.

"I feel pretty good, thanks. I needed that time off. It helped me process everything that happened these past few months," he replied.

"So, what do you think of the new digs then?"

Looking around, he nodded in appreciation. "It's an improvement on the boatshed. More room and more toys for the geek squad to play with no doubt."

"That's true, with the increase in budget we have a ton of cool new stuff, some even you will like," she said.

"Can't wait," he admitted, "So, what's so important I had to get here as fast as I did?"

"C will explain it all to you. He's waiting for you in his office," she told him. "I'll see you when you're done in there with him," she said, nodding her head in the direction of the office.

Seeing where she meant, he nodded in agreement, "Okay, see you in a bit then," he said and went to enter the office.

The interior of the office was identical to the old office. Chambers was not one for change. He worked according to the old adage that said, 'if it ain't broke, don't fix it' which he applied to most things in his life.

"Come on in Duncan, nice to see you looking so fit and well. I take it you have worked through all your issues and are ready to get back to work?" C said, then carried on without waiting for confirmation, "Good, because we have plenty for you to be getting on with, especially this incident on Altair, which is quite troubling."

Duncan stood in front of the desk, waiting for his orders. He waited until he knew his boss wanted him to join in.

"Which is what, exactly sir?" he asked finally.

"Something was stolen from a bio-genetics facility from the P5 containment area in their Black Vault. We are looking into the theft, which is difficult until someone there can gain us access to their computers so we can check their inventory."

"Why can't you ask someone who works there?"

Chambers looked at him before answering, "Because they left no one alive," he said.

Chapter 3

Altair

Marcus Raine was just getting started.

The theft in the bio-genetics facility was just what he needed to continue his plan.

Since childhood, he had been taught that the real inhabitants of Altair were the first settlers and that those who came later, in the time of the expansion, were interlopers and didn't deserve to live there. The expansion was when the Coalition was eager to find homes for the population of a dying world that had been chosen to be terraformed. The terraforming had begun, the facilities built and the atmosphere was beginning to formulate to enable human life to continue and thrive there.

Many more ships brought more colonists eager to start a new life. Then disaster struck.

In their haste to terraform the world into a living habitat, they had tapped into the core to use geothermal energy to run the huge terraforming plants. During this, somehow the core was fractured and volcanic activity began to rip the surface apart. Within months, the planet had ripped itself apart and the thousands of colonists who were able to evacuate found themselves homeless. The new start they had hoped for had been destroyed along with the planet.

The entire system became unstable as the destruction of the planet disturbed the stability of other planets, altering their orbits making it impossible for any of them to ever be used. In mankind's hubris in trying to form a world for their own ends, they ended up destroying one world and altering the orbit of eight other planets. Whatever alien life that had formed on these worlds that were suited to their particular environment were now also destroyed. It was an extremely severe price to pay and one that Raine held them responsible for.

Ever since that disaster, the Coalition had taken precautions that something like that would never happen again, but for Raine, it would never be enough. He now considered his world, Altair, exempt from the Coalition, in fact from the rest of the human race.

The focus of his anger and contempt were these interlopers, and he was determined to remove them from his homeworld.

Years in Altair's military had given him a set of skills he had put to use in the acquiring of the bio-weapon. He had covered his tracks by slaughtering everyone present. It was calculated to delay the authorities gathering any information about the incident and nothing more. He was well aware they would send someone to investigate, which was why he had taken such brutal steps to delay them. It was impossible to prevent them from eventually learning what had happened there. He just wanted to give himself enough time to complete his mission. By that time, it would be too late for them to do anything to stop him.

His privileged upbringing had also been a factor in his views. His family had always considered themselves entitled and nothing that threatened that lifestyle or privilege was ever considered acceptable and was always removed. In this respect, it wasn't difficult how he would come to think of the interlopers as being unworthy, literally beneath his consideration of even being thought of as human. At heart, he was a racist. He was white, powerful and bigoted against anything he thought unworthy of his attention. The family business had been his since the death of his parents, something he had orchestrated as he was unwilling to wait for their natural deaths to give him the money he so badly craved to continue his quest of destroying the interlopers. In that respect, his parents' teachings and views on others had brought about their own deaths. The irony of it all failed to even register on him though, he was simply doing what they had taught him; destroy anything that stood in your way to fulfilling your dreams and goals. They never expected those ideals to be their own downfall but in a strange and twisted way though, they would have been proud of him for doing it. Their own deaths were their greatest success because it proved all they had taught him had been worth it. He would be a formidable force to be reckoned with and not easily stopped from ever doing what he set his mind to.

Setting up a base hadn't been difficult. He simply used one of the business' factories. The one he chose was a munitions factory, which supplied arms to the military. There were certain areas of the factory that had been used to test new weapons. This was what he now used as his base of operations.

"Everything is in place sir," Mykel Robbins said as he stood next to him. Robbins was his second in command and a close friend. They served together in the Altair Special Forces. Raine was a Major and Robbins was his captain. They were both of similar height and build, both a little over six feet tall with well-toned bodies from their military service. They were like brothers in many ways. The only major difference was hair and eye colour, otherwise they could have been siblings. Raine had dark hair and eyes the colour of mud, whereas Robbins was lighter in both. His hair was the colour of sand and his eyes seemed to reflect the sky.

"Good, then we are ready to move forward. I'm expecting they will send someone to investigate the incident. I want the place watched and anyone showing up discouraged. Give them something else to think about, and it'll slow down their investigation giving us more time," Raine replied.

"Copy that. I'll get right on it," Robbins said.

As he left to carry out his orders, Raine sat at his desk contemplating his next move. He had started down this road and there was no turning back now.

Chapter 4

MI7 SecOps HQ, Terra II

"That was a bit dramatic sir," Duncan said. "They were obviously making a point."

"What, that they mean business? That part is obvious, but I think there's more to it sir. I think they were covering their tracks, giving us nothing to go on. Like all common criminals, they don't want to get caught, and they're doing everything they can to ensure that. This was just the start; we have to know what they stole. Once we know that, it'll give us a better idea of what their intentions are."

"I agree. I want you to go over there and take a look. See what you can find out about the place and what was being stored there. I've contacted the CEO of the company who ran the facility to get someone out there who can get access to their itinerary to see what was taken. They'll meet you when you arrive."

"Copy that sir. I'll do my best."

"We have no idea what sort of timeline we're working on here, Pryde, so do what you do, and do it fast."

"Will do, sir."

"Goodchild will forward all the details to your PIN. Your transport is waiting on landing pad five. Good luck and keep me informed."

"As soon as I have anything, I'll contact you with a sit-rep sir."

"Dismissed."

With that, Duncan turned and left the office. Goodchild was waiting for him when he emerged and said, "I've sent everything to your PIN, Duncan."

"Thanks Stef," he replied.

"Come back safe," she told him.

"It's just an investigation, that's all. What could possibly go wrong?" he said.

"Oh, there you go, you just jinxed it," she said with a head tilt.

"Don't go all sentimental on me. This is going to be just a walk in the park. I'll be back before you know it," he said then turned to leave. He hated long goodbyes, so he avoided them at every opportunity.

The landing pad where his ship was docked was one of the ten that the business they were using as a cover owned. He entered the small craft which powered up the moment he boarded. No one would notice just one more ship taking off.

"Welcome aboard, Commander. The destination has been uploaded from your PIN, the ship is prepared for take off and awaits your command," the female AI voice said from the hidden speakers.

"Glad to be back, Ship. You're operating as efficiently as ever I see."

"Are you flirting with me Commander?" the ship asked.

Duncan realised he was still operating in normal mode. He had a mission to complete so he concentrated on controlling his emotions. Dialling down his empathy, he was actively able to concentrate on the job at hand more efficiently. All his focus now would be on the job, nothing more.

"No Ship, that would be a breach of protocol as you know. Get ready to fire thrusters and take off," he said as he sat in the Captain's Chair at the front of the bridge.

"Copy that Commander."

As the thrusters fired, straps looped around him to keep him secure. As soon as the ship was in the air, the main engine kicked in and boosted the speed up to escape velocity within seconds. The inertia dampening field prevented him from being crushed to death. The screen in front of him darkened as they passed through the atmosphere up into space. The ship opened a window to hyperspace and it flew through.

The jump completed; Duncan saw the planet Altair looming large on the forward screen as they re-entered normal space. It was a bright blue orb in the inky darkness of space broken only by the pin pricks of distant stars. If it wasn't for the different formation of the land masses, it could be mistaken for Earth, the homeworld of the human race.

"Okay Ship, you have the address of the facility, take us in," he said.

Robbins had a team stationed near the facility, keeping watch on it. Three of his best men Clarke, Tatler and Summers, all ex-Special Forces, were given the job. They hadn't argued, even though they all thought that three of them was a bit extreme. Raine was not the kind of person to argue with if you valued your life, so there they were, waiting to see if anyone turned up.

Sitting outside of the facility in a camouflaged hide, the three men took turns watching through the camera set up that gave them an uninterrupted view of the entrance.

"Do we really have to do this?" Summers asked. It was his turn to keep watch, and he was beyond being bored.

"You have your orders, carry them out," replied Clarke, who had been put in charge.

All three of the men were used to working together, they had been a close-knit unit in the military and had continued after joining with Raine after their service had ended.

"Oh wait, I think we have some movement here," Summers said, drawing attention from the other two. Despite Clarke's assumed calm composure, he was as bored as the other two and any hint of some action was welcomed with renewed interest.

"Who is she?" Tatler asked.

A woman dressed in a dark blue business suit arrived by a shuttle that deposited her at the entrance then left in a hurry. She looked around then walked toward the facility.

The facility, due to the nature of the work they did, was located away from any city. It was situated in the middle of a small desert to the west of the second largest city on the planet. It had a wire fence surrounding it with gates that opened to allow road traffic through and a security system that was almost military grade guarding the perimeter. Nothing could gain access to the site without being spotted on any number of sensors.

"Whoever she is, she has access, so she must be someone pretty high up in the chain of command in the company," observed Clarke as they all watched her enter the facility.

"What do we do now?" Tatler asked.

Clarke thought about that for a second.

"Why is she here, I mean now of all times? The boss suspected they would send someone to investigate, what if she's here to help with that?" he said.

"What if she's the one sent to investigate?" Summers countered.

"Why not wait a bit to see if anyone else turns up before we go in there with guns blazing?" Tatler suggested.

"That's what I was getting around to," Clarke said.

"Works for me," Summers agreed, and they returned their attention to the screens just as another ship came down from the sky to land inside the perimeter fence at one of the landing pads.

"Here we go lads, something we can get our teeth into after all," Clarke said.

Chapter 5

"**K**eep things warm Ship, I'll be back soon," Duncan said as he prepared to leave the ship. He had chosen a pistol, his usual Walther Q9, along with two extra magazines which fitted nicely in clips on his shoulder holster hidden beneath his jacket. His PIN was in his pocket, and he was ready to go.

"Copy that Commander," the ship replied.

"Keep your sensors tuned to me just in case I run into any trouble," he said as he was about to leave. It was standard operating procedure in the service and was one of the reasons each operative was fitted with a chip. It not only facilitated such things as access to their bank account, but their ID as well, and it also served as a monitor. Because they could be tracked through the chip, it also gave access to their life signs. If anyone was monitoring their progress, they could see at a glance if they were in trouble of any kind, especially if they were injured.

"As always Commander."

Duncan closed the hatch after his departure and walked toward the entrance.

The heat hit him immediately as soon as he walked into direct sunlight, which of course, he had. He felt his skin begin to prickle in seconds from the intense heat. Looking at his wrist monitor, it showed the temperature at thirty-three degrees Celsius, and he increased his speed toward the cool interior of the building.

The door opened as he approached and he entered through.

The destruction from the attack was all around him. Walls had been blown apart as well as the roof being damaged. Bullet holes ran in patterns across the walls, more evidence of the violence perpetrated recently. There were blood stains on the walls and floor but the bodies had been removed to the morgue for the final examination before burial. It was a sickening sight, which was evident on the young woman's face, made even more shocking by her seeing no sign of emotion on his face. He was reacting as he would any other scene, with dispassionate objectivity.

The young woman facing him was in a dark blue suit. Long dark hair framed a face that was closed off and suspicious. Deep brown eyes stared back at him as he walked toward her. She was tall and slim, and the suit accentuated her athletic figure.

"I take it you're from the Ministry?" she said as she looked him up and down.

"Yes," he replied, which elicited a wide-eyed stare as her bewilderment showed.

"Is that it, are you going to let me know your name or anything?" she asked.

"Yes, I suppose I should. Pryde, Duncan Pryde, and you are?"

"Jessica Lyons, I've been sent to assist in any way I can."

"I need access to the facilities itinerary. I need to know what you do here and exactly what was taken. Can you help with that?"

"Yes, come with me and I'll show you," she said. Turning away from the entrance, averting her eyes from all the signs of destruction and bloodshed, she led Duncan inside the foyer and through to a series of offices. Everywhere was deserted now as the entire building had been designated a crime scene and wouldn't be given back until the investigation was over and the building deemed safe to return. In the meantime, only specific personnel had access to the building under correct supervision by an investigating officer. Jessica Lyons was obviously one of those.

The office she took him to was a large one on the ground floor and as she activated the computer Duncan said, "I expected the bio-containment areas would be deep in the lower levels below us.".

"That's right, all the actual work was done below. The intruders burst through the roof here, capturing everyone on the ground floor before working their way down to the containment levels," she replied.

"So, what do you think was stolen?" Duncan asked.

"I'm bringing up the itinerary now. We have several dangerous toxins and viruses stored in the different containment areas. According to the computer logs, everything is still here except for," she said as she read down the list of items stored in the containment storage areas. When her eyes landed on the only thing missing her eyes went wide and her jaw dropped open. "Oh my God no," she muttered when she saw it.

"What is it, what was stolen?" Duncan asked.

Turning to him she said, "Omega Five. They took Omega Five."

Duncan stared back at her; the sound of the item stolen actually sent shivers through him.

"Omega Five was banned several years ago. What was this company doing manufacturing that here?" he said.

"You have to believe me, I had no idea it was being stored here. Wait, you said manufactured, what did you mean?"

"All remaining samples of Omega Five were ordered destroyed after the Tannenbaum Incident. Either this facility was manufacturing it illegally, or they somehow managed to salvage one of the last remaining samples before it was destroyed and was storing it here. Whichever it was, it doesn't really matter, as both were against the order of the Coalition Council and therefore illegal," he said.

"This is bad, really bad, I am going to get fired over this, I just know it."

"I think there are more pressing concerns here other than your job," Duncan said.

Lyons shook her head then looked at him, "You're right, I'm sorry."

"Omega Five is the deadliest virus ever made. It was formed from some plant found on one of the first colonised worlds on the edge of Coalition space. Some bright spark designed it to be adaptable. It can target a specific genome in the DNA of a species making it the perfect killing weapon."

"Holy shit, what can I do to help? I'll do anything," she said. Duncan could tell from the way she wrung her hands and kept hopping nervously from one foot to the other, she was telling the truth when she said she had no idea about Omega Five.

"We need to gather all the data we can and check that no other samples of Omega Five are still here. What other monsters have they been working on or storing here, anything I should be made aware of?"

"No sir, Omega Five is the only thing that was stored here that was illegal. I'll download all the records to a portable device," she replied before getting to work.

"We have to ensure that this place is secure before we leave. Why is it not being guarded by the security services of your planet?" Duncan asked.

"I was told that it had been taken control of by an outside service, I thought you would be bringing some more people with you to take control of it all," she said, glancing over her shoulder to him.

Moving away, he accessed a comm channel through his PIN. He pressed his earwig implant to connect the call. When it was connected, he said, "Patch me through to C please."

"Chambers here, what have you found out?"

"It's bad sir, several samples of Omega Five were being stored here and that's what was stolen. Not just that though, the person who accessed the accounts for me told me she thought that others from my department would arrive with me to take charge of the security of this facility. Sir, it is empty, we need to make it secure before anyone else wanders in here to take a look at the goods."

"I'll get right on it. There is a Coalition Starship in your sector, I'll get it reassigned to take charge of the security for now until we can come up with a more permanent solution."

"I'll remain here until they arrive, Lyons is still downloading all the pertinent data about this place, so as soon as that's done and the starship arrives, I'll make my way back to HQ," Duncan said.

"Your priority Pryde, is to get back here with that data. The starship can handle everything else. As soon as you have the data, I want you to return here as soon as possible. Nothing else matters, is that clear?"

"Copy that sir," Duncan said and closed the call.

Returning to see how Lyons was progressing, he saw her standing by the table holding the data storage device in her hand. She was looking around nervously, her eyes darting around the room as if searching for something lurking in the corners of the room.

"Is that it?" he asked.

"Yes, it's all here," she replied.

Taking it from her hand he said, "We have to leave, you're coming with me."

Chapter 6

Outside the facility in the hide, the three men waited for the two figures to emerge.

Clarke said, "The moment those two show their faces, we strike."

The other two readied themselves for what should be an easy hit. They each had a Sabre G300 AAR, Adaptive Assault Rifle, configured in the sniper mode. It was chambered for the 6.8mm round which had been the standard military round for over a hundred years.

The two men with Clarke approached this part of the mission as a contest to see who fired first and who was most accurate. It helped to brighten up the dullest of assignments.

"Ok, here they come," Clarke said.

Duncan led the way out of the building and back out into the stark sunlight.

A glint caught his eye off to the side somewhere, and his instincts sharpened by years of training alerted him to the danger.

Pushing Lyons away from him and diving to the opposite side, he narrowly missed certain death as three high powered rounds passed between them. No sound was heard either because of the distance from where the shots had been fired from or the rifles had been fitted with suppressors, more than likely both. The glint he'd seen must have come from the telescopic sights fitted on top of the rifles. This had all the makings of a professional hit, so he knew they were in trouble.

They were out in the open with the only cover being his ship and there were at least two shooters out there, possibly more with sniper rifles. All he had was a pistol. He was severely outgunned unless he could get to his ship to even the score a little.

"What the fuck did you do that for?" Lyons screamed at him as she sprawled on the ground.

"Shooters, could be three of them, outside the perimeter fence," he replied which brought a wide-eyed stare of terror from the young woman. She was used to working in an office. This was not what she signed up for. "Oh my God, we're going to die," she whimpered, tears running freely down her cheeks.

"Not here, and not today," he replied.

Taking out his Walther Q9 from his holster, he jacked the slide to inject a round into the breach. Lifting his head up slightly from his prone position on the floor he tried to see through the fence where the shots had been fired from. When he was diving for cover, he looked for even a glimpse of a muzzle flash, but he hadn't seen any. This proved that the weapons had been fired using a suppressor so the most he could see would be the slight release of exhaust gases. Even that though, from this distance was impossible to spot. The only indication of where they had been was from the glint of sunlight off the lens of the sights fitted to the rifles being used, but there was no guarantee they would still be there.

He had to flush them out to try and even the odds a little.

Keeping low he said in a soft voice, "Crawl across the ground toward me and we'll make our way across to my ship."

Nodding her head, she tried her best to comply. Not ever having to crawl anywhere she had her behind up in the air as she used her knees and elbows to move her toward him. Had the situation been different and his emotions not been dampened, he might have found this amusing. As it was, she could get her behind blown off if she didn't lower it and fast.

Several bullets started to pepper the ground where they were as the shooters tried again to finish the job.

Realising this was taking too long, Duncan got to his feet and grabbed Lyons by the hand hoisting her to her feet also, then hauled her after him as the two of them made a desperate dash for the ship.

"Ship, target where those shots are being fired from and fire back," he said as he ran.

"Scanning now, Commander," the AI replied.

"When you have them, fire a warning salvo their way."

"Firing now, Commander," the AI replied, and the weapons systems came online. Rotary cannons dropped from recesses near the front of the ship and turned to where the three shooters were. A burst of shells tore up the ground in front of where they were hiding inside the camouflaged hide.

———

"How the fuck did he know where we are?" Summers asked when the bullets raked a path across the front of the hide. They had dropped immediately to the floor so as not to get hit should any of the large calibre bullets penetrate the walls of the hide.

"It's probably using heat signatures," Clarke said.

"Are you fucking serious, it's nearly forty fucking degrees out there, heat signatures my ass," Tatler sneered at him.

"Exactly you moron, the air-con in here probably showed us up as cold spots against the background heat," Clarke explained angrily.

"So, what do we do now then?" Tatler asked, not put off by the rebuke.

"If they reach that ship then we could lose them, so we stop them," Clarke said, already sighting through his scope before he started firing.

———

As the couple sprinted for the ship, bullets began kicking up dirt at their feet and whistled through the air narrowly missing them.

Lyons screamed in a pitch only dogs could hear as she ran for her life.

Duncan was almost at his ship when he heard his AI say, "Incoming."

Glancing across, Duncan saw a small object arcing toward them seconds before it hit the ground no more than ten feet from them.

The explosion hit them with enough force to lift them off the ground and hurl them several feet in opposite directions.

Duncan landed hard and rolled several more feet before coming to a stop. His clothes were torn and he felt pain from several parts of his body but he was still conscious, barely and more importantly, still in one piece. Being that close to an exploding grenade should have torn him apart. His head pounded from the concussive effect the explosion had on his eardrums and for a second or two he was disorientated and slightly deaf.

He knew he had to move or die where he lay, but just getting to his feet was a struggle. His balance was off and twice he fell back down to the ground.

Scrambling to his knees he looked around for Lyons. He saw her farther back closer to the building lying in a heap, not moving. There was blood on her face and her head lay at an unnatural angle, as did her legs. He didn't need to look further than her unseeing dead eyes to know there was no saving her. The explosion had killed her outright.

"Ship, target those shooters and end them," he said through gritted teeth as he tried to suppress his anger.

He was the cause of the death of a young woman. Had it not been for his getting her involved in this she would still be alive. He wasn't the one who detonated the grenade, or pulled the trigger, but he might as well have been. He was determined to make those who had, pay with their lives though.

Realising he had to get his feelings under control, he concentrated on that one task alone. Putting everything else out of his mind, he focussed on dampening down all his emotions, even his pain.

The ship targeted where the shots had been fired from, a disguised duck blind used by Special Forces as a hide, or observation post. It was camouflaged to be almost invisible.

The ship fired the rotary cannons directly at the hide with such blistering intensity the walls were shattered. The shells blew massive holes in the sides making it visible for the first time as the camo-shield was disrupted.

"Blow that thing apart," Duncan ordered and the ship fired a missile at it. The sleek projectile streaked across the space between the ship and the hide impacting the small duck blind and destroying it in an explosion that threw debris for over fifty metres.

Getting to his feet, Duncan was about to make his way to the ship when gunfire from three different directions forced him back down to the ground.

"Sonsofbitches," he swore when he realised they had escaped. Looking up from his position on the ground, he saw three men approaching, assault rifles aiming right at him.

Chapter 7

C larke had gotten them to leave the hide just in time.

They saw the rotary cannons tear up the front of their cover and he had ordered them out to tackle the intruder head on and on a personal level.

As they left their cover, keeping low, Tatler looked behind to see the walls disintegrate under the withering fire from the rotary cannons. The walls were literally blown to pieces as the large calibre shells blasted through.

"Holy crap, this guy is no ordinary investigator," he said.

"Move and keep the chatter down," Clarke ordered.

The three of them had just gotten clear when Summers spotted the missile from the ship.

"Incoming," he said, and they all hit the ground. The missile closed the distance between the ship and the duck blind in less than three seconds. The ensuing explosion destroyed what was left of the structure in a fiery blast that threw debris high into the air.

The shockwave hit the three men a glancing blow as they had minimised their profile by lying prone on the ground as flat as they could.

"Spread out, we'll catch him in a pincer movement," Clarke said as they left the hide.

Summers and Tatler went in opposite directions as they followed orders. They all had their rifles up and began firing as soon as they breached the perimeter fence of the facility.

"We got you now, you fucker," Tatler said as they neared their target.

Duncan looked up at the guys with the guns and remained calm. His Walther was still nearby and he rolled over to his left to grab it.

Bullets kicked up dirt where they traced a path between him and his gun. Jerking back his hand he rolled in the opposite direction away from his gun.

More bullets sprayed dirt in his face as they hit the ground before him stopping him in his tracks.

His only way out of this was to reclaim his gun to give him a slim chance of getting out of this alive. He rolled back toward his gun and this time he grabbed it.

Continuing his roll, as the three men carried on firing at him, he brought up the Walther and fired.

His first salvo of three separated the three shooters. They moved to accommodate better firing positions but continued their advance toward their target.

Time was running out for him. He had to reach the safety of his ship before they got much closer or they could pick him off with relative ease.

"Get him before he reaches his ship," a voice screamed. Duncan reckoned that must've been the one in charge. As they got closer he took careful aim and fired.

His first bullet hit the guy in front of him in the shoulder, spinning him around a little.

Springing to his feet Duncan moved closer to the ship for cover. Bullets from the soldiers struck the side just as he reached it.

So far so good, he'd avoided getting shot. Blood spilled from the cuts and abrasions from the explosion but he'd closed off his pain receptors, so it wouldn't slow him down.

The three men were now too close to the ship for him to use its armament against them. It was up to him now, he was on his own.

Moving around to the side, the other two men tried to gain an advantage on him. Duncan saw one of them appear at his side about twenty feet away. He had a clear shot on him, but Duncan fired first. His hastily fired bullet struck the man in the neck sending out a stream of blood as it tore through his carotid artery. The man's hand slapped up on his neck to stem the flow. Blood flowed quickly through the gaps in his fingers as his eyes went wide and he fell to his knees. He knew he was dying; Duncan saw the fear and shock in his wide-eyed stare as he looked at his friends for help that was never going to come.

The man who was still unharmed, worked his way to a better firing position around his other side, firing as he went.

Duncan dropped to the floor away from the bullets slamming into the ship's hull and the ground at his feet. Peering through the gap beneath the ship, he saw his attacker's legs. Taking careful, but quick aim, he shot him in his right ankle. The bullets shattered the ankle in a red splash of colour, collapsing his legs. The man fell on his side dropping his weapon. Frantically he reached for it, pain etched across his face from his shattered ankle and Duncan fired again shooting him in the face. The bullet smashed through the front of his forehead spreading his brains on the floor behind. His head flopped on the ground, a hole above his lifeless eyes.

Getting to his feet, he came out from his cover where the last man with the wounded shoulder was leaning against the side of the building, breathing hard and cradling his arm.

He tried to bring up his rifle and fire it one handed, but he found it difficult to aim. He fired but saw his bullets fly wide of their mark hitting the ship instead.

Duncan brought up his pistol and ended the fight with one bullet. The shot was on target and he watched unemotionally as the bullet took out his right eye as well as the back of his skull. The body dropped to the ground, all fight gone from him.

Looking around, Duncan searched for any more attackers. When he was certain that there were none, he climbed aboard his ship through the forward hatch.

"Ship, give me a damage report then get me out of here," he said as he flopped down painfully in the pilot's seat. He felt tired from the exertions and from his injuries sustained in the explosion. In his pocket, he reached for the storage device and felt relief at the sight of the undamaged device.

"The hull sustained some minor damage from the gun battle, Commander, but the self-repairing outer skin is already sealing the small ruptures. We are good to go. Where is our destination?" the ship replied. The AI controlling the ship's functions had already run a diagnostic and knew they could take off, which it had done as soon as Duncan was on board. By the time the full damage report had been completed and repairs were under way, they were already in orbit around the planet.

"SecOps HQ, Station Five. They need to see this data," he said.

"Course laid in. We can jump on your command," the AI reported.

"Okay, make the jump," Duncan said.

As Duncan's ship was about to enter the hyperspace window, he noticed another starship emerging from another portal. It was the starship sent by C to secure the facility. He felt relief that he had left the place in good hands as his ship disappeared through the hyperspace window.

Chapter 8

MI7 SecOps HQ

There was a medical team waiting for Duncan on his arrival back at the headquarters.

He went straight to Chambers' office, ignoring their ministrations and attempts to help.

"You look terrible Pryde, what happened?" C said as he entered his office.

He gave a quick run down of the events on Altair, especially learning about the Omega Five, and then handed over the storage device.

"Everything we found in the computer is on there, sir. You need to have a look," he said.

"I'll get the tech people onto it right away, you need to go with the medical team," C replied, taking the storage device from him. With a wave of his hand he said, "Go, go get cleaned up, then report back to me when you're done."

"Come with us Commander. Let's get those injuries seen to," Doctor Charles Willetts said as he came up behind and placed a reassuring hand on his arm.

Glancing over his shoulder, he saw the face of the calm doctor who was in charge of all medical matters. His dark eyes showed concern in how they narrowed.

"I'm fine Doctor, just a few cuts and bruises, nothing more," he replied.

"Come on, Commander. I'll be the judge of that."

"Go Pryde, do as the Doctor ordered and when you're done, we should have a lead for you to work off," C said.

With nothing left to do but comply, Duncan left with the medical team.

The new headquarters had a new addition, a Med Lab to which Duncan and the Doctor went to. Decked out in pristine white with the latest testing equipment situated throughout the spacious lab, it looked like the best hospital equipment.

"Sit down over there, and we'll get started," Doctor Willetts said. Duncan complied and sat on the bed, and Willetts took out a small medical scanner. In a few minutes, he had scanned his entire body.

"Well, no broken bones at least, which is a relief I suppose. I'll give you a dose of broad-spectrum meds that will help the healing process and protect you from any infection you might have picked up through those abrasions. I can treat the other things with a simple dermal stimulator," the doctor said.

Taking out a small injector gun, he placed it against Duncan's right arm and pulled the trigger, then he reached for a long tube-shaped device, which he pointed one end at Duncan's damaged skin. The end began to glow as the beam stimulated the skin cells into increased regeneration.

Duncan sat there patiently while the doctor worked his magic and when he put the dermal stimulator away, he said, "Is that it, are we done?"

"Yes, Commander, your skin will continue to regenerate. You should be back to normal in no time."

Getting off the bed he said, "Thanks Doc," and then made his way back to C's office.

"Come in and sit down. How're you feeling now, okay to get back to work?" C said as he entered. He took the advice and sat in the chair facing his boss.

"I'm good to go sir, or I will be once the meds kick in. It looks worse than it feels," he said.

"Okay, then back to work. The data you brought to us is being analysed as we speak, but it confirmed what you said about Omega Five. It seems they were manufacturing it under contract."

"To whom sir? It was banned and ordered that all existing samples be destroyed. That order came down from the very top, the President himself, sir."

C sat looking at Duncan not speaking for a second or two which actually said more than words ever could.

"The sneaky bastard," he said when the penny dropped, "To the public he said that he was safeguarding them by having this monster destroyed, but behind closed doors he was having it stockpiled."

"It appears so," C agreed, "Look, we don't have concrete evidence yet to work with but as soon as the data has been fully analysed, let's see what we come up with."

"In the meantime, we have someone out there with a batch of this stuff and the willingness to use it," Duncan said.

"Quite, so our first priority has to be finding out who took it and what they intend on using it for."

"Agreed sir," Duncan said.

"To that end, and considering the importance of this mission, I want you to work with a partner on this," C said, reaching for the intercom on his desk, "Send in Agent Sanchez," he said before Duncan could argue.

"With all due respect sir, you know I work best alone," he said as he heard the door close behind him, clearly the agent in question had entered and heard everything he said.

Coming to stand next to him, Agent Sanchez said, "Don't worry, Commander, I'll try not to get in your way too much."

He glanced at the person who had spoken, because the voice had surprised him. What he saw was a tall woman dressed in a white blouse with dark blue trousers. Her jet-black hair was long and lustrous which at the moment was pulled back from a smooth forehead into a tight ponytail at the back of her head. She kept her gaze fixed firmly on the man sitting in front of her, affording him only a profile view. Her nose was slender and not too long and her lips were full and pressed together as her jaw was set in either determination or annoyance at his reaction to her inclusion to this operation.

Clearly, she was used to being dismissed as an agent, even in these times when females featured more in the frontlines than ever before. There would always be those who thought they couldn't carry their weight though, and Duncan had proved he was one of those.

"Commander Pryde, this is Agent Veronica Sanchez who will be your partner on this mission. I want you to work together on this. It is too important for a solo mission," C said.

"Again sir, with respect, I work best alone," Duncan reiterated. He was still in mission mode, so his empathy was dialled down along with his other emotions, and he was still blocking his pain from the injuries he sustained in the recent gunfight, so he was indifferent to his comments being insensitive. He really and honestly didn't care at that moment. Later when he allowed his barriers to open up, he would realise what an asshole he was being, but not now, and not here.

"Do I look like someone who gives a damn what you want Pryde. I've made my decision, now deal with it," C replied harshly, cutting off further debate. He was well aware of Duncan's ability but at times like this, a direct approach was the only way to deal with him.

"Copy that sir," Duncan said, knowing there was no need to pursue this any farther. Chambers had made his decision and there was no going back.

"Good, now before you leave, go and visit the armoury. Since our budget increased, we've been able to procure some new weapons. The Armourer has your new sidearms. I suggest you go, pick them up and familiarise yourselves with them," C said, then dismissed them both.

Duncan stood up and without acknowledging his new partner, turned and walked off.

Sanchez stood there a little unsure of what had just happened, looking from C to the door where Duncan had just left through.

"What are you waiting for, an invitation? Go after him, you're his partner now," C said without looking up from his work.

Chapter 9

The Armoury was in the lowest section of the new headquarters. When the two of them arrived, Sanchez halted at the door placing a hand on Duncan's chest to stop him from continuing.

"Okay, I get it. You're used to working alone. You don't like change. I get that too, but we've been ordered to work together, so why don't we try to make the most of it. After all, it's not like it's a permanent thing," she said, looking up into his deep blue eyes.

Duncan returned her gaze dispassionately.

"You miss the point; I work alone because I know I can trust myself. I don't have to worry about a partner getting into trouble. I just have one thing to concentrate on and that's the mission. It's more efficient that way, it's nothing personal," he replied.

"You don't have to worry about me. I can look after myself," she assured him, which was unnecessary as he said, "Don't worry, I won't," and then he walked past her into the Armoury.

Inside the room were a row of firing ranges at the far end with stacks of shelves that held an alarming array of pistols and rifles with the accompanying magazines. Not only that but there were other shelves with other weapons on such as rocket launchers, grenades and other munitions.

Duncan looked around at them all as he stood in the doorway, wondering who was in charge of all this.

"So, you finally found your way down here then," a voice said from off to the side. A reed thin man in a dark shirt and trousers came out to greet them. He was in his mid-fifties with slicked back salt and pepper hair. He held himself stiff, a military bearing that told of his years in the Special Forces.

"Major Thomas Booth, I like your new digs," Duncan said.

Major Booth was the armourer for SecOps, but his old department was much smaller than this new one. Here he could indulge his love of all things technical as pertained to weapons.

"Yes, it's much better than the old place, and I have the next gen weapons for you and your partner," Booth said which brought an immediate rebuke from Duncan.

"We're not partners," he said.

"Okay, moving on," Booth said as he saw the look both gave him. He moved off to one of the racks to pick up two pistols and brought them over to the firing ranges. "Okay, these are to be the new standard sidearm for this department, well all of the Ministry really. The Coalition Defence Force will also be adopting it so you'd best get used to it."

"What are they?" Sanchez asked as she picked up the small pistol. Ever since the twenty-first century, pistols had not evolved much in the respect of design nor the type of ammunition used. The pistol that Sanchez held in her hand was simply the latest in that long line of modular design that had begun almost two centuries ago.

"It is the new SAP10. Manufactured by the Security Armaments corporation, the SA denotes the name of the corp and the P stands for Pistol, in case you were interested. This weapon is basically an upgraded model of the Q9 but with a few differences. The main one being that instead of the previous round, this pistol is now chambered for the new 10mm round. These new rounds are fitted with hardened tips to maximise their effect. Everything else about the new pistol is very similar to the Q9, so you shouldn't have too much difficulty in getting used to it. This new round being slightly larger will mean that the magazines can't hold as many rounds, fifteen, sixteen if you have one up the pipe. The change to this round was made purely to increase stopping power, one hit from these bad boys will make any hostile think twice about continuing the fight."

Duncan and Sanchez both picked up their respective pistols, inserted a mag into the butt and faced down the range. He took his stance then fired off a few rounds at the distant target. Each bullet struck the target then blew a hole as big as a fist in it.

"Impressive," he said when he saw the damage being done. "Okay, I think we're done here," he said eager to get back to work.

"Wow, this is some toy," Sanchez said from the range next to him, obviously she too was impressed with the new weapon.

"We haven't finished yet my boy. There is a bit more to go through before you get to leave," Booth said, stopping him in his tracks.

"What else is there to know?" Duncan asked.

"Give me your full attention and I won't keep you longer than an hour or two," Booth said.

"You're kidding," Duncan said.

Booth looked at the two of them for a second, his expression giving nothing away. A smile creased his face, lighting it up and he said, "Actually, yes, I am. I just wanted to see your faces."

Duncan gave a slight head tilt as he couldn't see what the purpose of it was. Deciding there was nothing to be gained from further conversation, he simply said, "I'll be leaving now."

Back in Chambers' office, he was greeted with a stern-faced expression that told him they had little to go on.

"I see that there was not much gained from the data to help us," he said as he sat down in front of the desk. This time there were two chairs placed in front, and Sanchez took the one next to him.

"Oh, there was plenty of data alright but nothing that helps us to identify who perpetrated the attack and theft," C replied, his lips pressed firmly together a clear sign of his frustration.

"If I may sir, what is the significance of Omega Five?" Sanchez asked, leaning forward slightly nervous that she had to ask this question.

"You gave me a partner who hasn't been fully briefed," Duncan snapped coldly, almost bouncing in his seat.

"Apologies to the both of you. I was going to brief Agent Sanchez at the appropriate time, which seems to be now, a little late, obviously but there it is," C said a little sheepishly, which was not at all like him, Duncan noticed. He relaxed as he noticed that his outburst shouldn't have happened. Normally in mission mode, he was in total control of his emotions and nothing bothered him, ever. So, why did this elicit such a vociferous reaction from him, and why now?

"Omega Five is a particularly nasty retrovirus. Without going into too much detail, retroviruses work backward in a host going from RNA and turning that into DNA and hence infecting the host. That is a basic explanation, these retroviruses have been tamed though, so that instead of harming the host, something that can help heal can be introduced into it, and therefore work to the host's advantage. In Omega Five's case, it can be modified to target a specific host, whether it be a single person in a crowd or an entire species or gender or ethnic minority. It is untraceable and so far. We have found no way of stopping it once it has been deployed nor treating the infected once that has happened. This was why it was banned and ordered to be destroyed. It seems we failed," C said.

Duncan came out of his reverie as C finished his explanation.

"Who do we think might have use for a weapon such as this sir?" he said, getting back to the task at hand.

"What are you getting at, Pryde?" C asked.

"Why Omega Five, I mean it is a specifically nasty weapon that has a specific ability. Is there anyone we know who would benefit from the use of such a weapon sir?"

"Good point."

"Also, sir, how did they get to know that it was even there? The security around it had to be of military grade proportions. It's not the kind of thing that you would freely advertise."

"Agreed."

"Did the CEO of the company sound afraid when he was told of what had happened, how did he react?"

"Now that you mention it, he seemed as if he almost was expecting the call."

"What is the CEO's name sir?" Duncan asked homing in on a possible lead.

"Marcus Raine."

"I think we need to have another talk with him sir," Duncan said.

"I agree. Get over there right away, I'll arrange a meeting with him for the both of you. Be careful, if he is involved in this in some way, there's no telling how he'll react if he thinks you're on to him."

"Copy that sir," Duncan said, getting to his feet. He glanced at Sanchez, "Come on, we've got work to do," he said, acknowledging the fact he had a partner for the first time.

Chapter 10

Altair

Marcus Raine looked at Robbins, not quite understanding what he was hearing.

"What do you mean you lost contact with the team?" he shouted angrily.

"The comms went down hours ago. I've been trying to re-establish them ever since," Robbins replied. He paused, looking down at his feet then said, "I think I know why we lost contact."

"Are you going to tell me, or do I have to guess," Raine snapped at him.

"We picked up a sensor signal from orbit. A starship is parked over the area, and they sent down a shuttle. There is a contingent of CDF Marines now at the location. I'm not sure what they're doing there, but it can't be good," Robbins said.

"Well, it's obvious your men failed in their task. They're either dead or captured, and we need to find out which it is. If they're captured, we have to be sure they can't tell anyone what happened there."

"How can they, they don't know anything. I wouldn't worry too much about them. It was why I chose them. They weren't involved in the original incursion of the facility. All they knew was what I told them, that there would be someone sent there and they were to stop them learning anything or leaving with anything they had learned."

"Okay, but I think it's time to move up the schedule," Raine said to which Robbins agreed. "I'll make the necessary arrangements."

As he moved off Raine, was left thinking about his situation. His determination hadn't diminished. He was concerned about not stopping the investigation though. He had wanted them to be delayed, which would give them time to complete the final stages for what he was planning. Now it seems that might not be the case.

A call came in from his aide back at the business headquarters.

"Go ahead," he said.

"Sir, there is a meeting that's been set up between you and an officer of the Ministry. I thought it best to comply otherwise they might start to think we had something to hide, sir," the aide said.

"Damnit, I don't have time for this," he snapped.

"With respect sir, if you don't take this meeting, it will look like you are involved. At the very least it will look like you have something to hide," the aide said.

He thought about that for a moment. Maybe he could put them off by taking this meeting, maybe lead them in the wrong direction.

"Okay, you're right of course. Send me the details to my PIN, and I'll make sure I'm there."

The starship was waiting for them on a landing pad as they left the headquarters. It was a small, sleek craft that had the main engines at the rear with secondary engines placed on struts at the back horizontally.

The bridge or flight deck was at the forward section protected by triple hull configuration with deflector shields as well as main shields to protect the ship. It had an impressive array of armament for such a small craft, and it was controlled by an AI that interacted with Duncan almost as a member of the crew.

"Do all agents get a ship like her? She's a beauty," Sanchez said when she saw her for the first time.

"I don't have an answer for that," he said honestly.

They boarded the ship and Duncan said, "Ship take off please and set course back to Altair."

"Copy that, Commander. Please take your seat. Welcome aboard Agent Sanchez, make yourself comfortable please," the Ship replied, which further impressed Duncan's partner. She took a seat on the bridge next to him with a broad smile on her face.

Duncan had noticed her elation and asked, "What's with the smile?"

"Don't you feel anything when you come aboard a ship like this? She is special. A ship this size that can run with minimal crew like she does is exceptional. Most ships need a crew of at least four possibly more but this virtually runs herself."

"It does run itself and no, I don't feel anything when I come aboard. This ship is just that, a ship, nothing more than a tool manufactured for me to do my job more efficiently."

The Ship replied, "If I had feelings, Commander, I would be hurt by that remark."

Sanchez looked at Duncan a little harder, her eyes narrowing slightly as her gaze was more probing than she gasped, "You're him, you're the one I heard about. The agent who has no emotions," she said, adding, "I thought it was just a rumour, you know, like an urban legend type thing, but you're him, aren't you?"

"No," Duncan replied. Normally this type of questioning wouldn't bother him but for some reason, Agent Sanchez was having an effect on him and he had no idea why. Suddenly, he felt he had a need to explain and said, "I have emotions, everyone has them, except sociopaths who often mimic them to fit in with company. Psychopaths have no empathy nor remorse and often are highly intelligent, as are sociopaths, and they often see themselves above others and therefore the normal rules and laws don't apply to them. I am neither of those, although I do have some traits of a sociopath. I can turn my emotions on or off at will when the situation demands. It helps me to perform more efficiently but to say I have no emotions is completely wrong, and I don't know why I'm telling you this."

"So, let me get this straight, if we get into a tough spot you wouldn't hesitate to sacrifice me if the mission warranted it?" she asked.

"Yes."

"Without hesitation?" she asked, needing clarification although from his stoic expression she already felt she knew the answer.

"Yes," he replied immediately.

"Wow you didn't even stop to think about that, did you?"

"What is there to think about, the mission comes first. If it means that to save millions of lives, I have to sacrifice yours, then the choice is simple."

"What if it's a choice between me and one other life, how do you make that choice?"

"By weighing up the advantages to success of the mission. Whichever results in the mission being a success is the choice to make. The mission comes first."

"Sometimes it isn't as easy as that though."

"Why?"

Looking away, Sanchez knew that this argument was going nowhere and she suddenly felt the beginnings of panic flutter deep in her stomach. A premonition of dread filled her as she realised her chances of returning from this mission were not good.

All further conversation died as the ship deployed thrusters to lift them off the landing pad before the main engines boosted their speed to escape velocity, and they were speeding through the clouds up into the upper atmosphere and out into space.

Once the jump through hyperspace was completed Duncan said, "Okay Ship, take us in to land."

Chapter 11

"What's our plan here?" Sanchez asked as they reached the corporation headquarters of Raine Shield Corp. It was the first time she had spoken since their conversation on board the ship.

Duncan had disregarded her attitude as he was trying to remain on focus for the mission. It was increasingly difficult for him to block out his emotions, which was confusing for him. Was he developing feelings for this woman? He had known her for less than a day and yet somehow, she had managed to crack his composure. If they stayed together for any length of time, he was actually afraid she might destroy his barrier completely. He had to finish this mission fast so he could return to working alone.

"We go in and question Raine, learn what we can about his involvement in all of this and then report back to headquarters."

"Sounds like a plan," she said, adding, "nothing likely to get any of us killed."

They had landed on the rooftop landing pad of the tall building. It was an edifice of gleaming metal and glass that stood tall above the other buildings nearby asserting its dominance over them. It was a statement that said I am more important than you, a testament to the ego of the man in charge.

An elevator took them from the rooftop down to the Penthouse suite of offices where Marcus Raine reigned supreme over the rest of the workers employed there.

As they were shown into his spacious office that had walls of glass affording him a view over the city this building dominated, Raine was seated behind a desk in the far corner positioned there to give him an unobstructed view over the city.

"Please come in, I hope this won't take too long as I have important matters to attend to," he said, remaining seated.

"Thanks for agreeing to this meeting sir," Duncan said, "I promise not to keep you too long, as long as you answer my questions truthfully."

"Excuse me, what do you mean by that?" Raine said bridling at the thinly veiled threat.

"Exactly what I said sir. What did you not understand by it?"

Duncan saw the man at the desk visibly calm his reactions and relax a little more. He had hit a nerve right off the bat, but he wasn't sure just yet if it was because he had something to hide or if he was simply swamped with work which the break in at his facility had increased. Probing further would clear it a little.

"Now, what do you know of Omega Five being manufactured at your facility?" he asked, continuing his investigation.

There was a pause and Duncan could see in the way Raine fidgeted in his seat that he was uncomfortable about this. He waited, figuring that the longer he allowed the question to hang there would add pressure to answer.

"You have to understand I was only doing what he ordered us to do. I mean, what was I supposed to do, after all he is the President?" he said, finally holding his hands out in supplication.

"Are you saying you were acting under orders from the President himself to manufacture Omega Five?" Duncan asked.

"That's exactly what I'm saying, yes."

"You do realise he's on record ordering the destruction of this virus and the further manufacturing of it has been made illegal under penalty of death?"

"Of course, that's why we had to keep it away from prying eyes and off the grid. If anyone learned of this, then we would all suffer."

Duncan stood back a little. Something about this didn't ring true. Why did he give in so easily?

"You'll forgive me for being a little sceptical here. It is a little strange that you would offer this up so fast. You didn't even try to deny any of it. In fact, I never even had the chance to accuse you of anything yet."

"What's the point? You obviously know it was illegal to make the damn thing, I mean who doesn't so trying to deny it would be stupid, and I am not a stupid man."

"That's up for debate," Duncan chided.

"What's that supposed to mean?" Raine asked his anger bristling under the surface.

"Well to agree to this in the first place is not the act of a wise man, wouldn't you agree?" Duncan elaborated.

"Point taken, but it would have been career suicide for me to refuse. The power that man wields means he could destroy me and my business with one call. I literally had no choice."

"We all have choices, Mister Raine, and you chose to protect yourself rather than do what was right, a little like what you seem to be doing right now," Duncan said, still not convinced all of this was correct. He still felt he was being played.

"Oh, so not only am I stupid but a coward as well, is that what you're saying?" Raine said.

"I didn't say that sir, you did, but now you mention it." He let the words hang in the air like that as he looked him directly in the eye. He could almost see the seething rage hidden, tethered behind a layer of what was thinly disguised civilised behaviour.

Raine finally said, "If we're done here, I would like to return to work. There is an enormous amount of crisis management I need to tend to because of all of this. If there is anything else you need, kindly direct your questions to my secretary, who will be only too pleased to accommodate you."

"Thank you for your time sir," Duncan said then the two of them left the office.

The two of them returned to the rooftop in silence.

"What just happened in there?" Sanchez asked when they reached the rooftop. She waited until they were out of the building before asking for fear they were overheard.

"That, Agent Sanchez, was a display of misdirection, elegantly done I might add. It was pure theatre, well-rehearsed and impeccably played but theatre nonetheless."

"So, you're saying he lied to us?"

"Oh, most definitely. But about what, that is the question."

As they boarded their ship Sanchez asked, "So, what now then?"

"Now we find out what he was lying about," Duncan replied.

Chapter 12

Raine watched the two agents leave his office and he relaxed a little. He hoped he'd sent the one who did all the talking off in the wrong direction. Time would tell. No doubt there would be further questions but by then he would be too far down the road for them to do anything about stopping him.

He seemed cold, trying to get to the truth, or what he thought was the truth, with an efficiency that bordered on obsession which, he had to admit, he found worthy in an opponent.

The woman was completely different. She was cute to say the least. She had a good figure, curves in the right places and those lips were for kissing and all that hair, what he wouldn't have given to see it cascading across the pillow next to his after making her his own. Putting thoughts like that out of his head, he returned to the business at hand. He didn't have time for fantasy, he still had work to do and he couldn't do it sitting behind this desk.

Getting to his feet, he made his way out. On his way, he said to his secretary, "Hold all my calls, if those agents call back, I'm not to be reached. I've instructed them that you will answer their questions. Is that understood?"

"Perfectly sir," his secretary replied from behind her desk. She had been working for him for over a decade and probably knew more about the daily running of the business than he did. She could handle two nosy agents from the Ministry in her sleep.

Riding the elevator up to the rooftop landing pad, he emerged to see the other ship taking off.

"Wonder where he's off to?" Sanchez said when she saw Raine exit through the door on the rooftop. There was one other ship on the landing pad when they had arrived and now, they knew who it belonged to.

"Ship, is there any way you can track that ship?" Duncan said.

"Activating tracker now, Commander." As the AI said that, a small magnetic device was fired at the other ship. Too small to notice unless you were looking for it the tracker covered the distance between the two craft in less than three seconds. It was directed by the AI and attached itself to the under hull of the ship Raine was heading for out of sight of anyone near it.

"Take us up and put us in orbit for the time being. I want to see where he's going," Duncan said.

"Copy that, Commander," the AI said.

"Did you pick the voice?" Sanchez asked.

"Pardon me?" Duncan said, wondering where that had come from.

"The AI has a distinctive female voice, quite sexy in fact. I was wondering if you had any input in choosing it, that's all."

"None, it came with the ship," he replied.

Sanchez smiled knowingly as she said, "Of course it did."

He ignored the smirk and instead replayed the conversation in his head.

"Commander, the ship has taken off and is headed for one of the munitions factories on the edge of the city," the AI said.

"Keep a track on him, let me know where he ends up at," Duncan said.

"We need to report this to C," Sanchez said.

"Agreed," Duncan said, then said, "Ship patch me through to MI7 HQ."

When C came on the call Duncan said, "Sir, we spoke with Marcus Raine and he is certain that President Harada was the one responsible for them manufacturing Omega Five. He claims Harada ordered him to go ahead and to keep quiet about it. Sir, we need to challenge him about this."

"Well, this is interesting, I wonder what his response will be. I'll contact him right away. You remain with Raine. I have a feeling he knows more than he's letting on," C said.

"Copy that sir, we'll remain on station until you've spoken with President Harada," Duncan said and closed the call.

"Where are we going then?" Sanchez asked.

"Might as well follow Raine and prepare to move," he replied.

"I've a better idea, why not get a hotel room and grab a bite to eat. We can then decide how to proceed. We need more information on what Raine is up to if he is in fact involved in this. We can do that by breaking into where he went to once we have the address. By that time, C will have spoken with the President and we'll have a better picture about this. What do you think?" Sanchez suggested.

Duncan looked at her and said, "Okay, it seems like a good idea, and we do need to eat."

"And once we're done we can get some sleep before reporting back to C. If we have time, that is," she said.

"Let's see what we can learn first. That might force us to act sooner than we know."

"Agreed," she said.

"Ship, take us into the city. Find the nearest space port and put us down there," Duncan finally said.

Chapter 13

C contacted President Harada via video link. When the call was connected, he said, "Thank you for taking this call Mister President and I must advise you to go secure."

Harada narrowed his eyes in suspicion for a second before reverting back to his friendly face as he complied.

"Go ahead William. You can talk freely," he said.

C could tell from the connection that the call was not being recorded and was indeed secure.

"Mister President, I wonder, have you been made aware of the break in of a bioweapons facility on Altair owned by Marcus Raine?" C asked to begin with.

"Yes, I have been advised of it," Harada replied tentatively.

"In that case, you must also be aware of what was stolen."

"Why would you assume that?"

"Because Marcus Raine told us that you ordered him person-ally, to store and manufacture the item that was stolen," C said, he kept his attention focussed on the president's face for any signs of deception. This was why he chose to call him on the video link.

"Are we talking about Omega Five?" Harada asked.

"Yes, we are Mister President."

"And Marcus said I ordered him to store and manufacture it at his facility?"

"That is also correct sir."

"Then I suppose it would be difficult for you to accept that his version of events differs from mine."

"I would expect nothing less sir."

"In that case, it's just as well that I kept a log of our discus-sions about it then, isn't it?"

"You have proof that Raine lied about his version of events?" C asked, expecting as much. He knew well how wily and devious the President could be, and with something as poten-tially dangerous as this, he would definitely cover his back.

"I am, you see, it was Marcus who suggested to me that we don't get rid of it. I sanctioned his corporation to be respon-sible for the destruction of the virus, but he said that it was too valuable to dispose of in its entirety. He said that he could store it safely and even manufacture more of it in case it was needed some time in the future," Harada explained.

"And you agreed to this, even after seeing the results from the Tannenbaum incident, you still thought it a good idea to keep this?" C said, trying to keep his voice under control despite the anger he felt.

"The galaxy is a dangerous place William, you more than most know that. I made a decision to safeguard our planets and the people living on them. Was it a bad decision, possibly, but I did it in good faith. Who hasn't made bad decisions for the right reasons? We're all capable of doing it, even you William," Harada said proudly. Like all politicians, he was never going to admit to doing something wrong, even in the face of overwhelming evidence to the contrary, he would still try to rationalise it with a statement that he was doing it for the good of the people.

"You're right Mister President. The galaxy is a dangerous place, unfortunately, your decision to continue with the Omega virus program made it even more dangerous."

"Well then, now is the time for you and your agency to earn all the extra funding I gave you. Go out and find whoever is responsible for the theft and stop them from using it," Harada said, then abruptly ended the call.

C sat in front of the monitor fuming in anger, his fists balled on the desktop. He couldn't believe the gall of the man. Not only did he not feel any shame for what he had done, but he was not willing to take any responsibility either. In his opinion, he obviously thought he had done nothing wrong and then something dawned on him as the detail of the conversation he had overlooked suddenly came to light.

It wasn't Harada anyway, but Raine. It was Raine who had suggested keeping the virus and manufacturing more, but why? What had he got in mind, he wondered?

He would have to inform Pryde and Sanchez about this development as it would change the way they looked at this mission.

Taking a moment to focus his thoughts, he made the call.

Chapter 14

Altair

The city, New Amsterdam, was the capital city of Altair, and therefore the largest and most visited by off-worlders. It was the centre of trade and business on this planet, and the population of this one city was rising at over six million.

It was a dense city with buildings seemingly crammed in tightly to minimise space and utilise every square foot available. Most buildings had more than twenty floors and many had over a hundred.

The hotel Duncan chose was the Imperial and was right in the heart of the city, giving them full access to a staggering number of restaurants and bars. Taking adjoining rooms, Duncan took little notice of the comfort offered by the room. Each room had a lounge with seating for at least two people. The bedroom leading off it was en-suite so they each had their own shower. Once they had checked in, they chose a restaurant across the street from their hotel for convenience only.

It was a restaurant that had a French influence. The long dining room had tables down each side running the length of the room with a centre aisle that had tables in between at intervals to break up the uniformity and give it character.

Once seated, they decided to order from the cocktail menu. Duncan chose an Old Fashioned with a fine aged Bourbon and Sanchez a Paloma, which had a local Tequila as the main ingredient, while they perused the food menu.

As they read what was on offer, they remained quiet, Duncan preferring not to engage in small talk.

When the waiter returned with the drinks, they had chosen what to have to eat.

Duncan chose the Chateau Briand cooked medium rare with all the trimmings while Sanchez preferred the pan-fried sea bass with lemon, garlic and herbs.

They drank in companionable silence, neither of them wanting to speak first.

When the food arrived, they began to eat.

"This is really good, I mean really good," Sanchez said, breaking the silence.

"I agree," Duncan replied. He added, "Have I said something that upset you, you've been quiet since we landed?"

"What do you think? You more or less told me I am expend-able to this mission."

"That's not what I said but you are, though. The same as I am. It comes with the job; the mission always comes first."

"How can you be so cold and calculating about it?" she asked, keeping her voice low so the other diners wouldn't overhear.

"Years of practice I suppose."

"Well, it's good to know you have my back in this," she said, her words dripping with sarcasm.

"You have no need to worry, I do have your back. I will do everything I can to protect you because you are an asset to this mission. With you working with me, the odds of success have doubled."

As he watched her, he saw her expression relax a little. The thought of her impending doom must have been playing on her mind, which was something that had never occurred to him.

"If only I could be sure about that," she said, averting her eyes from his.

"You can, we are partners after all. We began this together, we'll finish it together," he assured her.

At that moment his PIN chimed in his pocket. He touched his earbud to activate it and said, "Go ahead."

"We've done some digging into Raine's past. It seems he is ex-military and took over his family business after the death of his parents. It was just a few months before the Tannenbaum Incident, and just after the relocation of the immigrants were placed on Altair from Cygnus III. Raine was vociferous in his comments about the immigrants and how they didn't belong. It is looking more likely that he has some involvement in this," C said.

"Thank you, sir, we intend on getting into his factory tonight to see what we can learn from it," Duncan said.

"Be careful, Pryde, until we have confirmation that he has possession of the item, we still have no proof he is involved, so tread carefully."

"Copy that sir," Duncan said and the line went dead.

He looked across at Sanchez and said, "When we're done here, we are on the move."

Sanchez looked at her drink and said, "That means no more of this until after we're done then."

"When they had finished their meal, Duncan pressed his forearm against the table sensor to pay the bill via the chip implanted there. It showed his ID as the same as the one he had booked in at the hotel under, Robert Frost, a cover ID which his chip could rotate to any number of IDs with all the background information required to give a good cover story.

As they got up to leave, he said, "Let's get back to work."

Chapter 15

"How are things progressing, Doctor?" Raine said to the smaller man hunched over the instrument on the desk before him.

Looking up from the eyepiece of the nano scope, Doctor Abraham Silkin saw his employer standing at his shoulder. He'd been so engrossed in his work, he never heard him enter. Returning his eye to the sculpted eye piece he said, "As well as expected but slower than I'd like with all the intrusions and interruptions. Things would go a lot smoother and much faster if you just allowed me to continue without these continual visits."

"The situation has escalated, Doctor. Therefore, so has the timeline. I need you to have it ready, well actually, now would be nice," Raine said, keeping his voice calm and measured despite the anger building within him over the disrespect shown to him by an employee.

"Impossible, these things cannot be rushed," Silkin said, looking up defiantly at him.

Raine returned his gaze with one that instantly made the doctor regret his insubordination, "You have one hour. Make it ready or lose your life, your choice," he said, holding his gaze a little longer before turning and walking off.

Silkin watched the man leave the lab, and he let out the breath he'd been holding in as he wondered just what he had gotten himself into here. The doctor was an expert in viruses and was the obvious choice to perform the task of altering the Omega Five virus to strike a specific target. He had shared some of Raine's views, especially on the immigration issue, but not for the same reasons though. His reasoning was that Altair was already reaching its maximum population level, to suddenly have thousands more dropped on them would overload the already stretched ability to feed them. Relying on outside sources for food was never a good idea, especially from another world for if the supply chain ever broke down, for whatever reason, it left those relying on the supplies dangerously unable to cope. Any world must be able to sustain its own population, otherwise they were on a path to self-destruction. To this end, he had joined in with Raine and his vision to safeguard the indigenous population of Altair.

He knew Raine was determined, centrally focussed on his one purpose, but he had no idea just how laser-like that focus was. Everything was a stepping stone to him, something that must be overcome in order to go forward, even those who worked for him on the same goal. He had just witnessed it first hand, and he was afraid for the first time since joining this project. He had always considered himself to be integral to the success of the operation, without him Raine would never succeed.

If he had been honest with himself, he had never for a moment thought Raine would actually use the virus. He had considered what he was doing was nothing more than a threat. What he had said to him had chilled him to his core though. He wasn't as important as he had thought. Clearly, he was the only person capable of doing what needed to be done to complete the operation, or so he had thought. His own ego had led him to believe he was invulnerable and everything hinged on his ability to get the job done. Now, it seemed he was wrong. He didn't know how, but the look in Raine's eyes had left him in no doubt that if he didn't do as ordered within the hour, he would surely die. It also made him think that his earlier assumption could also be wrong. He could actually be planning on using this virus.

If that was the case, then he would be guilty by association but what could he do, he didn't have the testicular fortitude to stand up to this man. His choice was clear, he had to comply.

With this new incentive in place, he returned to his work with a renewed vigour.

After the meal, Duncan and Sanchez returned to their respective rooms and made preparations to leave.

They gathered their things together separately and when they were done, Duncan settled the bill with the hotel.

"Where to now?" Sanchez asked as they walked back to the car park where they had left the vehicle they had arrived from the spaceport in.

"Now, we go pay Raine a visit," Duncan replied as he opened the boot of the vehicle to throw their bags in.

Standing back, Sanchez looked at it with a slight head tilt.

"What?" Duncan asked.

"Being a spy and all, I thought you'd have a flashier car, you know. Something like a sports roadster or something, not this," she said, indicating the car in front of them. Her expression was of disappointment, as if he'd let her down.

"How many undercover ops have you been on?" he asked.

She looked at him, her brow dropping over her eyes as she wondered what that had to do with anything. "This is my first, I came straight from tactical," she said.

"Well, the first order of business when working undercover is to be able to blend in," he said.

"Well trust me, no one will look twice at you driving this piece of shit," she said.

"Exactly, now can we get in and get on with the job?" he said.

The two of them climbed aboard and as she sat in the passenger seat she said, "I get your point but if the shit hit the fan and we had to make a run for it, I doubt we'd get very far in this thing."

"You'd be surprised, she has a few tricks up her sleeve. She's a bit of a wolf in sheep's clothing," he said with the hint of a smile.

Duncan was right, although the car they were in was built around the basic chassis of a Nimbus, a mid-range ground vehicle manufactured by the Sabre conglomerate who not only manufactured a series of cars but also shuttles as well as fighter aircraft, it had been upgraded. The bodywork had been replaced with hull plating, the windows were the same as on a starship and the power cell was boosted with a fusion drive cell capable of reaching speeds of up to two hundred kph. The power cell and upgrades meant it was one of the safest vehicles on the road. Apart from that, it had defence and offense capabilities too.

The work had been carried out by the talented staff at the Ministry and was one of a fleet supplied to certain agents in the field, Duncan being one of them.

To the casual observer it was a simple run of the mill Nimbus saloon car but in truth it was as Duncan had described a true wolf in sheep's clothing.

Leaving the car park Duncan steered the Nimbus through the city to the facility where they had traced Raine to. As night drew close and darkness began to shroud the city in its cloak of anonymity, they proceeded toward answers to questions they had yet to ask.

Chapter 16

Raine kept an eye on the time. He'd given Silkin an hour to complete the task he'd been set. That hour was almost up.

He set off back to the lab walking fast. Things had accelerated fast and he was eager to get his mission on track, but to do that, he needed Silkin to finish off his work.

"Tell me you have finished, Doctor," he said as he stormed into the lab.

The smaller man looked around and said, "I have just completed the last tests to complete the final stage of the procedure."

"Does that mean you have or you haven't?" Raine said impatiently.

"Yes, I'm done," Silkin replied.

"Good, good, then we can finally get started," Raine said. "Get everything sent over to the launch section," he said, "We are about to begin the eradication of the intruders," he finished before leaving. He set off, heading for the launch site which was on the same floor, the ground floor at the rear of the complex. The launch area was where all the testing of weapons were conducted. He had made preparations already for what he planned on doing and everything hinged on the virus being made ready in time.

He reached the section in less than a minute and smiled when he saw what he'd done. It wouldn't be long now; all he had planned was about to come to fruition.

"Okay people, get ready. I want this first test firing to go as smooth as silk. No mistakes, I want nothing to go wrong with this. As soon as we get the results of this one, we can move on to the big one. Let's go people, get to work," he said to everyone present. The moment he stopped talking, there was a flurry of movement as they all dropped what they had been doing to change tasks to the one now most important.

Raine watched as he knew they were about to make history.

The road ahead was clear once they left the city limits. The AI installed in the car was linked to the one controlling the starship, so it was easy to pass data from one to the other.

Inside it was spacious and the dashboard was clean and tidy with all the instruments displayed in front where the driver had easy access to.

Duncan allowed the AI to drive until they were clear of the city before he took over manually.

The munitions factory was away from the city for obvious reasons. When the city receded behind them, the roads became less well travelled until it became a simple single-track road seemingly leading to nowhere.

The headlights on the Nimbus lit their path as night closed in around them.

On the horizon they saw lights from the compound where the factory was. Duncan turned off the headlights and proceeded in the dark. The car was equipped with night-vision capability that was connected to the windscreen. It acted as a Heads Up Display so that they could see in the dark.

Trees lined the sides of the road as it cut through a forest and Duncan pulled up the car a few hundred metres from the compound hiding it in the forest.

The two agents were dressed in fluid body armour combat suits that covered them from head to toe. A hood was pulled tight over their heads which contained a visor that had night vision capability. Around their waists they wore a belt with pouches and a holster for their pistol. They set off through the trees toward the compound treading as softly as they could. Keeping low to minimise their profile, they proceeded slowly to their target.

They conversed silently through a com link connected through their PINs where their earbuds gave them the audio feed. When they subvocalized, their voices carried through the connection.

They reached a perimeter fence, which was over ten feet tall, and stopped.

Looking all around, Duncan saw the electrodes atop the fence posts which told them the fence was electrified. It probably carried enough of a charge to kill anyone stupid enough to get close enough to it. Taking out a small device from his belt he extended a telescopic rod and hoisted it up to the electrode on the right. He gently placed the small item on top of the electrode and then brought the thin rod back down. He placed another of the small items on the tip of the rod and repeated the action with the electrode face first. Putting the rod away, he activated the two tiny devices which dropped a small screen in front of the electrode which cut the signal to the fence on this one panel without sounding any alarm.

Duncan indicated to Sanchez to stay clear as he took a small laser cutter from a pouch in his belt and started cutting a hole in the fence. The two of them crawled through the hole in the fence and continued on as stealthily as they could toward the factory.

A grassy lawn stretched out from the edge of the trees they were in toward the compound. Open ground covering more than two hundred feet lay between where they hid on the edge of the trees and the walls of the compound.

Duncan signed for Sanchez to keep low. He had tapped into the security feed via a wireless connection through his PIN. On the screen he scrolled through the surveillance cameras routine. In a few seconds, he knew where and when the cameras would cover the area they were going to cover. The security feed also informed him of how many guards there were and where they were stationed. From that, he learned their routine of patrolling the grounds.

He soon had a window of opportunity which he entered running across the lawn he led Sanchez toward the compound's wall.

Reaching the wall, they crouched down below a window. This would be their point of ingress. Accessing the locking mechanism on the window with his PIN, he inserted the code to open the window. A quick look inside told him the room was empty so they progressed inside.

Duncan closed the window behind Sanchez and said, "Okay, we're inside, that's the easy part."

Chapter 17

Now that they were inside the room, they had to decide where to go next. Duncan's priority now was learning everything he could about Raine and if he had the Omega Five virus and if he did, what he intended on using it for.

He couldn't do any of that from inside the room. He had to get out of there and find somewhere where this information was stored.

The room was a simple storage cupboard, probably for the janitor. Mops and buckets and cleaning products filled almost every space available. A rack of shelves lined one wall filled with said cleaning products.

Duncan pried the door open a crack to see what was out there. There was a corridor that passed by from left to right. Duncan popped his head out to take a better look and it was clear.

"Follow me," he said, waving Sanchez on after him.

At the end of the corridor, they came to a row of open plan offices. Everywhere was quiet and deserted. All the workers had gone home, this was the legitimate business section of the factory. What they needed was obviously in another section of the facility.

"We need to go deeper," he said.

"You mean inside this building?" she queried.

"No deeper as in, down below. Chances are, what we're looking for will be down below out of sight of the normal day to day running of this place," he said.

An elevator was close by with a door at the side. He opened it carefully to see a staircase that led in both directions, up and down.

"This might be our best way down, the elevator would alert them," he said.

"I'm with you," she said.

Slowly at first, they made their way down the stairs with the knowledge that at any moment one of the guards could appear through one of the doors leading off the landings at the forefront of their minds.

On the way to the compound, Duncan had looked over the schematics supplied by his ship's AI after a quick search on the local databases. It had given him a rough idea of the layout only, there were no details of what was one each floor, just the basic layout. From that he extrapolated that anything they wanted kept hidden, would be on the lowest floor.

The stairwell was dimly lit at this time of night, only a skeleton crew would be working so the chances of running into anyone was minimal, at least that's what they hoped.

Once they reached the lowest level, they opened the door slowly. It opened out onto a short corridor that had three doors leading off it.

There was one facing them and one on either side. Choosing the one to the left Duncan opened it a fraction and saw an office that had glass walls looking out over a large open space.

"I think we may have struck it lucky the first time," he said quietly. He went through into the office and over to the desk. On the top was a computer which he opened up accessing the files using a universal unlock code which bypassed any security measures in place.

He took out a small storage device and inserted it into the computer. It was recognised by the operating system and he began to download all the files he found onto it. He could go through them all later when they were clear of this place. He'd seen enough in his first glance through them that what he needed was all there.

The download complete, he took out the thumb drive.

"We're done, time to go," he said.

Sanchez had stood by the door keeping lookout all the time he was downloading the data. When she heard he was done, she nodded her affirmation.

The instant he shut the computer down, an alarm sounded throughout the entire compound.

"We just ran out of time," Sanchez said.

Chapter 18

"What the fuck was that?" Raine asked when he heard the alarm. It was hypothetical because he knew there was only one reason the alarm would sound, because they had an intruder.

Robbins was with him at the launch site going over everything with him prior to the launch.

"I'll go check it out," he said as he turned to leave.

"Make sure you catch whoever it is. I want to know who they are and how they got in here," Raine ordered the retreating figure. Robbins held up a hand to say he would do as ordered without stopping. He knew there was no point in trying to talk to him when he was in this mood, not so close to the finish line as they were.

The launch site was on the lowest level, the same as the office Raine had been using as his own. Although it was on the same floor as the office, it was at the opposite end. Robbins left the launch site and ran toward where the alarm had originated from. His PIN had indicated the exact location, and he was running as fast as he could, calling more guards to converge on the office.

A feeling of dread filled Raine as he thought about what the consequences of this break-in could be. How did they even know there was an office down this far from the rest of the facility? The only thing he could think of was that, whoever they were, they must have learned about them having the Omega Five virus, but how?

He had been sure to cover his tracks. Oh sure, he knew someone would come to investigate eventually, but he'd also put steps in place to delay any investigation. Seems like his tactic hadn't been as successful as he'd hoped.

He just hoped Robbins got to them in time.

As he entered the office, he went to his computer. It didn't take long to find that there had been a download of all his files from this computer. He was furious.

"Secure this office," he said to one of the guards who had arrived shortly after him. To the others he said, "Go up top and assist Robbins. Whoever was in here must be found."

Storming back to the observation centre, he saw through the large window that all the work had stopped.

"Carry on with the countdown, nothing must stop the launch," he said to the technicians who were all looking around to see if they should evacuate. Raine waved his arms enforcing his earlier order. When that failed to motivate them, he drew a pistol, a Mak S10 and aimed at them.

"The first person to move get's the first bullet," he said, which seemed to provide the correct amount of motivation as they all returned to their tasks.

Robbins met up with more guards close to the office where the breach had occurred ahead of Raine.

Whoever had been here was long gone. He activated the internal sensors which were connected to every camera in the compound. Using the office as a starting point he soon found what he was looking for.

"Right, people get moving. They're heading for the surface and a way out of the compound. I want them stopped," he said, not just to those with him, but to the rest of the security staff still on the premises.

They wouldn't get very far, not now he had them in his sights.

Duncan and Sanchez had left the office as soon as the alarm sounded. Not bothering with being spotted on any surveillance system now their only priority was to escape.

Sprinting up the stairs, they left caution behind and concentrated on getting clear of the compound before security found them.

As they reached the ground floor and burst through the door, they were met with a barrage of bullets.

"Whoa!" Sanchez screamed as they both backed into the stairwell. Bullets slammed into the door, tearing up the surface of it but not quite penetrating it. The fire door held firm even against this mighty onslaught.

"What do we do now?" she asked.

Duncan didn't reply, simply took out a grenade and primed it.

"Nice," Sanchez commented when she got the idea.

Duncan pried the door open just enough and tossed the grenade as far as he could given the gap he had to work with, then slammed the door shut once more.

The explosion on the other side of the door shook it so violently that Duncan felt the pressure wave slamming into it. He silently prayed that it would hold, which it did.

When the blast was over, he opened the door and went through into the office area they had first searched. Many of the work areas had been destroyed by the blast and he saw at least two bodies lying in a bloody heap, an arm over by his left, a leg over by the wall, torn apart by the explosion.

"Come on, if they knew enough to send these goons here then we might have to fight our way out of here," he said.

This was nothing like a 'quick in and out' that he had originally planned.

They moved fast and as they rounded a corner, they almost ran into a group of armed guards.

Duncan backed away immediately, shooting the first guard he saw. Other guards fired back, missing the two agents.

Holes appeared in the walls where bullets struck sending chips and shattered pieces of pumice flying into the air.

Duncan and Sanchez fired around the corner, cutting down enough of them to force them to seek cover inside one of the offices nearby.

Changing direction Duncan and Sanchez retraced their steps as they made their way to the janitor's closet where they had infiltrated the compound. Duncan hoped they wouldn't think to look here, but it was a long shot and definitely more appealing than trying to fight their way out of the main entrance.

Everything had been like they had left it and he told Sanchez to watch the door as he opened the window to see if there were any more guards out that way. The open ground beyond was as he'd hoped it would be, clear.

"Okay, let's go," he said, going through the window. He crouched down at the side of the open window keeping his back against the wall, watching for any signs they had been spotted as his partner followed him out of the building.

When they were both out, he said, "Right, keep low and run for your life."

Sanchez didn't need any other incentive as she set off at a fast sprint followed by Duncan who kept his attention split between what was in front and what was behind them.

They were halfway to the cover of the trees when a voice behind them shouted, "There they are, open fire."

The next second Duncan felt something slam into his back sending him tumbling off his feet as bullets filled the air.

Chapter 19

Raine watched the countdown close to the end. His eyes went from the timer to the window from which he could see the tiny rocket that would be the first step in his plan of eradicating the interlopers from his homeworld.

This was just the first step, to test the potency of the virus. When the results were in from this test then he would move on to the full attack to finish them all off.

"Sir, where do you want the sample going?" asked a voice behind him.

Raine turned to look at him, his eyes narrowing in confusion. "What sample?" he asked.

Holding a small container in his hands, the technician said, "This one sir."

His eyes strayed to the window where the rocket blasted off and his face blanched, all the colour drained from it.

"What sample?" Raine asked once more, this time more forcefully.

"The sample that had been altered sir," he said, then he realised what had happened.

"Oh shit, oh fuck!" he said shaking in fear.

"What did I just send up in that rocket?" Raine asked, almost afraid of the answer.

"The samples must have gotten switched sir. This is the sample that should be in that rocket."

Raine spun around to look at the smoke from the rocket's engine trailing high into the sky before levelling off to its final target destination.

"Then what the hell did I just send up in that thing?" he said.

In a quivering voice the technician said, "The original sample, maybe, sir?"

Raine knew what that meant, it was a disaster and a fatal one at that. Without the virus having a specific genetic target, it would affect anything it came into contact with. That one small sample could effectively wipe out all life on the planet.

"Abort, destroy that rocket," he shouted.

"Sir, you insisted on it not having an abort system fitted into it. There's no way we can stop it now," a voice from down in front answered.

He knew this anyway. His own insistence on ensuring nothing would or could interfere in his project once it had begun was to be his final undoing.

Just like those he despised for killing all those innocent lives, he had now become one and the same. He had signed the death warrant of every living thing on his homeworld.

Dropping into a chair, Raine held his head in his hands as he stared at the window which the launch pad could be seen through.

"What have I done?" he asked no one.

Duncan rolled with the blow, getting back to his feet in an instant. He returned fire at those who had shot him, thankful his fluid body armour had prevented any harm coming to him.

His shots were off target but he never expected them to hit anyone, merely to make them think and pause giving them more time to reach the hole in the fence.

Glancing up, he saw Sanchez standing by it firing at the guards who were chasing them, giving him covering fire.

The guards were not put off for long and soon after Duncan turned back to make another run for it, more bullets started flying past him. The shells came so close he could feel one almost singe his cheek.

Firing behind him without even looking, he ran as if the hounds from Hell were on his heels.

Finally, he reached the fence as more bullets hit the mesh close to him. Turning one last time he aimed and fired hitting one of the chasing men, dropping him which gave the others pause for thought for a second only as they stopped in their tracks to aim and fire.

Duncan pushed Sanchez through the fence then followed through himself. As soon as they were clear, they sprinted to his car. Once inside it, Duncan activated the defence systems then started the engine.

Gunning it, the almost silent power cell thrust them forward, forcing Duncan to wrestle with the steering wheel to control the skid. Turning the car around he pointed it back toward the city and the space port.

Sanchez breathed out in relief.

"We made it," she said.

Robbins reached the ground floor as the guards were firing at the fence.

"Damnit, they're getting away," he snarled through gritted teeth. Through his comm link he said, "Get a chopper in the air right now. They must have arrived in a vehicle, so I want it stopped. Kill them if you have to, but they do not leave this area. The rest of you get after them in cars."

"We're not out of the woods just yet, no pun intended," Duncan replied.

Just then, large calibre shells blasted through the canopy of trees that had given them some semblance of cover, sending up masses of dirt as they struck on either side of the car.

Someone was firing at them through the trees from above.

"They don't give up easily, I'll give them that," Sanchez observed a little anxiously. Despite the danger they were in, she found herself enjoying it a little. Whether it was purely the danger she liked or that she was facing it with this enigmatic man who intrigued her, she was not clear which it was. She decided it could wait anyway, until they were out of danger.

One thing she was certain of was that she was glad she was facing this with Duncan. He was the perfect agent to have at your side in a crisis and he was certainly living up to his reputation.

"They are persistent," Duncan agreed. "Car, target that vehicle above us and see if you can't dissuade them from continuing their attack," he said.

"Copy that, Commander," the car replied in the same voice as the one used by his ship's AI.

A small pod emerged from the front driver's side hull, just to the rear of the wheel arch and turned to point up through the trees. The pod had several small, but extremely powerful, rockets with quantum warheads. No larger than the size of a pea yet powerful enough to take out a jet copter, the rockets were a deadly addition to the car's armoury.

"Target acquired, Commander," the AI reported.

"Fire," Duncan said, and the rocket was set loose streaking up through the treetops to strike the craft that was following them.

The explosion could be seen clearly through the trees as fiery debris began to rain down behind them. Sanchez turned in her seat to view the spectacle.

"Wow! That was awesome," she said with a broad smile.

Their satisfaction was short lived though as gunfire from the rear peppered the back of the Nimbus. The car shuddered from the impact of so many bullets striking it and Duncan strove to keep her from going into a deadly spin.

"What now?" Sanchez asked, turning back to face front in her seat.

Duncan ignored her comment and instead concentrated on the job at hand. Activating the rear guns, he opened fire on the trailing vehicles.

The two small mini rotary cannons spewed an astonishing barrage of bullets at the first car, an All-Terrain Vehicle with large thick tyres. The shells tore up the front of the grille shattering the engine beneath the bonnet sending up thick smoke that billowed in front blinding the driver. The ATV veered off crashing into the trees on the roadside killing all those inside.

The other two swerved around the crashed vehicle and continued with the chase. More bullets were fired at the retreating car striking the rear with as much effect as before.

"They don't learn very quickly, do they?" observed Sanchez.

Duncan remained silent, his focus was on escaping, nothing more.

One of the vehicles gained on them and came up alongside, smashing into the passenger side door in an attempt to drive them off the road.

Duncan pushed the wheel over to compensate pushing back against the other vehicle. Bullets struck the back of the Nimbus as the other vehicle was right on his tail giving him no respite.

The ground was uneven and all the vehicles bounced around which made controlling them even more difficult.

Pushing the car at the side of them away for a second, Duncan was able to pull ahead and put some distance between them. More bullets struck the side of the Nimbus as the other vehicle tried to come up on that side.

Divots of dirt were kicked into the air at the side of the Nimbus as bullets raked the ground on that side.

"This is getting tedious," Duncan said.

Selecting incendiary grenades, he fired one at the nearest vehicle chasing them. The grenade impacted the front of the car and exploded in a fireball which soon engulfed the entire car. Flames destroyed the car from outside trapping the passengers inside. Soon the car exploded when the power cell overloaded trying to compensate for the increased temperature as well as trying to fight the flames.

The explosion lifted the wreckage thirty feet into the air then it crashed down on the forest floor. The impact burst the car sending out further flames and debris blocking the road. The last car had to swerve through the trees avoiding the burning wreckage to re-join the chase. By this time Duncan had increased their lead and was almost out of sight.

As soon as Duncan saw the last car emerge from the trees back onto the road behind them, he fired a rocket. The explosion destroyed the last vehicle chasing them and he increased his speed wanting to put as much distance between him and the compound as he could.

He had a feeling that time was running out, but he had no idea just how right he was.

Chapter 20

The small community that Raine had targeted was just one of the encampments chosen by the Coalition Council to house the immigrants. There were several more, but this was the first and mainly acted as an induction camp for anyone who had been placed there.

Although it was the first, it only housed a few hundred in permanent housing while others who arrived later, and were still arriving, were sent on to the larger communities which were growing on a daily basis.

The organisation of allocations was overseen by a delegation from the government of Altair. The three-man team was stationed there on a rota basis, their tour of duty was about to come to an end and they were due to be replaced by another team.

"Sir, we have a small object approaching the base, too small to be a craft," warned Hydecker who had been manning the sensors. They had had to deal with some of the locals who had been against the number of immigrants allocated to their world and had petitioned against it as well as demonstrated around the perimeter. It had gotten bad enough that the organisers had erected a fence to keep everyone not authorised to be there, out.

"What is it then?" Sommerley asked, a little annoyed at the intrusion. He was planning to get away tomorrow and had been finishing off the few final details before leaving at first light.

"Well, it's too small to be a craft of any kind."

"You said that already Hydecker. Get to the point man," Sommerley snapped angrily.

"That's just it. I have no idea what it is."

"Oh, for fuck's sake man, let me take a look."

Sommerley strode over, his arms dangling at his side like a petulant teenager. "What am I looking at?" he asked, wanting to get this over with so he could leave.

"There, that thing," Hydecker indicated, pointing at the small sensor screen on the wall of the room.

Sommerley stiffened as he saw the object tracing a path directly toward the compound faster than any small craft had a right to.

His fingers danced over the sensor controls, inputting data and extrapolating references to get a clearer picture of what they were dealing with, until finally he stood back. His face was ashen as he read the results of the deeper scan he had just completed of the object.

Looking at Hydecker he said, "It's a rocket, and it's heading right for us."

Duncan was approaching the city when his AI said, "I am reading a launch of a rocket from the factory we have just left, Commander. It is heading for the immigration entry point, five thousand miles from here."

Duncan continued driving, keeping his focus on completing this part of the mission. He had succeeded in getting information from Raine pertaining to the theft of the Omega Five virus and that was what was important at this time, nothing more.

"Did you hear that, they launched," Sanchez said, staring at him. From the pitch of her voice, he knew she was angry and frustrated that he was not showing more emotion.

"We did our part, we got what we came for and now we have to ensure that information reaches the right people. I can't think about anything else right now, the mission is clear and I'm going to carry it out no matter what," he replied.

"What about the launch? Aren't you going to do anything about it?" she asked furious at his seeming nonchalance over it.

"What exactly do you have in mind?" he countered.

"I don't know, something, anything."

"Well, until we know for certain what he is planning on using the Omega Five for, there's not a lot we can do about it. There's no proof that whatever he launched has the virus on board. My first and only priority now is getting this data to MI7 HQ so they can look it over and decide what course of action to take."

"The launch has ended, Commander. Whatever it was containing has now been delivered," the AI said with even less emotion that Duncan had displayed.

The rest of the journey to the space port was carried out in total silence. When they got on board, Duncan ordered the AI to set course back to Terra II.

As they took off Sanchez asked, "Is it possible to see if you can find out anything about that launch? See what happened?" her voice was low and filled with sorrow. In her heart, she knew whatever was on that rocket people had been hurt, or worse and they had done nothing to prevent that.

The AI was silent for a few moments as it steered the ship up through the atmosphere and into position to make the jump to hyperspace before finally saying, "The launch carried the Omega Five virus. The rocket exploded above a small compound dispersing the virus into the atmosphere."

"That makes it even more important we get this data to the right people," Duncan said as he listened to the report. He guessed the AI was not finished though. "What else is there, Ship?" he asked.

"I am reading changes in the atmosphere over the compound Commander. The virus that was delivered was just a tiny sample but from the readings it had not been genetically altered in any way."

"Is that important?" Sanchez asked.

Duncan knew the importance of that but when he spoke, his voice showed none of it.

"It means that without a specific genetic marker to target, the virus will target anything in its path."

"Oh," Sanchez said thinking about it. She went quiet for a second as the importance of what he had said sunk in.

"Wait, are you saying it will kill everything in its path?" she asked, still not believing it all.

"Yes, I'm saying it will kill anything in its path, that includes people, plants, animals and the entire land will be devastated. Omega Five will kill all life on this planet if it's not stopped even down to the microbes in the soil. Nothing will survive, now do you get why it's so important to get this data to the right people?" he said.

Sanchez went quiet as the importance of what had just happened permeated through her mind. This was more than just important; this was life and death important.

All further conversation ended when they went through the hyperspace window back to Terra II.

Chapter 21

Altair

Hydecker saw the rocket more clearly now as it loomed above their heads. Just as he was about to head for shelter, the thing exploded in a huge fireball.

Debris from the blast began falling to the ground forced outward by the force of the blast followed by a fine mist that spread out even farther.

The clear mist descended on the compound like a summer rain shower. In the dark it was almost impossible to see but the effects were instantly felt.

Hydecker felt the delicate touch of the fine mist as it landed on his face as he looked up trying to see a little better. Others who had joined him in looking up to see the rocket also felt the mist on their skins.

Elation ran through the onlookers. What they thought at first was going to be a disaster turned out to be nothing more than a little shower. Elation soon turned to irritation though as the effects began to make themselves known.

Irritated at first, they tried to rub it off but couldn't. The mist was carrying the Omega Five which was quickly absorbed through the pores of the skin or breathed into the lungs. It penetrated through any method available to it, quickly attaching to cells in the host altering and ultimately destroying until the only thing that was left was the virus itself.

Within seconds of it first touching their skin, people were beginning to feel the effects. Some developed a cough while others began bleeding from noses, eyes and ears. The ground beneath their feet began to dry up as all plant life sucked moisture from the soil to try and prevent their own death.

Shrivelling up and withering away, plants and flowers and even the grass, were seen to be dying off almost before their eyes. Panic spread through the compound as people started to realise they were under attack but from an invisible source.

Within the first half hour people began dropping, within the next half hour almost all of the inhabitants of the immigration compound had died and the ground all around was drying up in death as well. Spreading out the virus killed everything it touched and would continue until there was nothing left.

News of the attack was quickly brought to the attention of the government by a call from Duncan as they departed. He had instructed the ship to send a message with all the relevant data to them so they could immediately affect a rescue protocol. The military was deployed with incendiaries to scorch a wide perimeter around the compound as a firebreak to halt the virus' advance. When it was completed, they stood back as huge shield generators were positioned around the scorched firebreak to form a defensive barrier around the entire compound to prevent the airborne virus from escaping that way.

The action had been hastily carried out, but it was effective and the virus was stopped in its tracks. A guard was set up to keep watch over the area to ensure it remained secure and to prevent the idiot faction from trying to investigate inside.

For now, they had it under control.

Chapter 22

MI7 HQ, Terra II

"Reports are just coming in about the strike on the compound on Altair," C said as they entered his office. They had stopped off on the way to hand the data storage device to the IT department for them to download everything from it.

"Anything of value, sir?" Duncan asked.

"Well, so far they're trying to keep a lid on just what happened. They are saying that the incident is not dangerous and they are investigating to learn the cause of it."

"Which is political speech for they know exactly what it was, but they don't want to start a panic," Duncan said.

"Quite right, the damage done was minimal considering what was released," C was saying when Sanchez interrupted.

"Minimal, how can you even say that, sir?" she said, then realised her outburst was insubordinate.

"I can because it's true, Agent Sanchez. Considering the amount of Omega Five that was released and the swift action taken by the authorities, thanks to your call Pryde, we are lucky not to be looking at the extermination of all life on Altair and not just a few hundred, sad as that might seem. Once the authorities were made aware of the threat and how dangerous it was, they were able to scorch the earth around the site and erect a barrier over it to prevent it finding a new host outside of the compound. Had they failed, they would have been facing the total annihilation of all life on their planet."

"I'm sorry, sir," she said standing to full attention in front of the desk.

"No need to apologise, Agent. I understand where your concern came from, and trust me when I say that you are not the only person to feel like that."

"What happens now, sir?" Duncan asked.

"Well, it's obvious to everyone now who was responsible. We traced the rocket launch to one of Raine's factories, where you gained that data from. We have issued an arrest warrant for him and asked for his bank accounts to be sequestered and any travel ID to be rescinded. He won't be going anywhere. There is also a tac team headed for the factory to take control of it and to take back and destroy all other samples of the Omega Five virus."

"So that's it then sir. The mission is over then?" he asked.

C smiled a little then said, "It is indeed Pryde, it is indeed. There are a few details to be cleared up, such as capturing Raine and the virus, but I'm sure the Altair security forces can handle a simple job such as that. You and Sanchez can go and enjoy a few days off. You've both earned it."

"Thank you, sir," Sanchez said, smiling in relief. Duncan was not so sure though.

"If it's all the same with you sir, I'd rather remain active just until this is finally cleared up," he said.

"As you wish, Pryde. I'll keep you informed of any progress," C said with a wave of his hand dismissing the two of them.

Chapter 23

Altair

When the Altairan security forces arrived at the factory, Raine was long gone. All they found were bodies of the security staff who had engaged the two agents in battle and the morning workers wondering what was going on. They had arrived thinking today was just like any other day only to be met by a cordon with armed security forces barring their path.

Raine had evacuated the place along with Robbins and a few of his men who were there, taking with them the other samples of the Omega Five virus. He knew they would be coming for him after the debacle that was the first test. Still, he took some solace from the fact that at least some of the immigrants had been removed from his homeworld, even if it had been only a few. He was dismayed though that he had destroyed part of his sacred home planet in his rush to get things done. That was unforgivable, and he swore it would not happen again.

He knew they would be coming for him and would spare no effort in finding him, especially considering what he had with him. When they learned he had disappeared and had taken the Omega Five with him, they would increase their efforts to find him.

It would be almost impossible to find a safe location anywhere on the planet he so dearly loved, not with the sophisticated sensory equipment at their disposal so it was with a heavy heart he chose to leave.

He had many starships at his disposal so getting off world wasn't a problem, getting off before they issued a notice of no travel on him would be the problem, so he had to act fast.

Gathering everything he needed and his loyal followers, they boarded one of his ships while others were also ordered to leave with different destinations logged into the planetary Flight Control database. He became a veritable needle in a haystack.

By the time the authorities had realised he had left, they had several hundred ships of his to search through as well as the normal traffic that came and went from this world on a daily basis.

Chapter 24

MI7 HQ Terra II

It was late in the day when the news of Raine's departure reached C's desk. The information had been delayed as they had continued a fruitless search trying to locate him and the virus.

By the time C heard about it, Raine had been gone for more than half a day, more than enough time to give him a credible head start.

"It seems you were right not to leave, Pryde," he said after calling him into his office. Duncan had stayed behind, going through a search of all of Raine's properties while he waited for what he considered the inevitable news. He had been proven right on this occasion, which he took no pleasure in.

Once he had finished his search, he tried to grab a quick nap, but the chair wasn't conducive to the requirements of a good night's sleep so when he appeared in C's office, the dark circles under his eyes were evidence of his growing fatigue.

"You look awful man; did you get any rest at all?" C asked concern, furrowing his brow.

"Some sir, so I suppose we don't have any idea where he went then?" Duncan replied, brushing aside the concern. He would rest properly when Raine was captured and the Omega Five was stabilised or destroyed and not before.

"I'm afraid not. By the time they realised he'd vanished, there was no way to track him. The crafty bugger had arranged for scores of his ships to leave at the same time as him with a variety of destinations logged in to Flight Control. By the time they had gone through all of those, he was long gone. Quite clever if you ask me," C reported with just a hint of a smile which showed his respect for the intricate planning.

"We already know that he's adept at strategies, sir. His military training took care of that. We have to out-think him now, predict what he will do next and take into consideration that he'll be thinking the same thing too and will plan ahead for our moves. This is like a game of chess. We have to plan three or four moves ahead because that is what he'll be doing," Duncan said.

He was blaming himself for not finishing the mission, for focussing on getting the data to headquarters rather than stopping Raine. If he had taken Sanchez's advice, then perhaps none of this would have happened. Sure, the disaster at the immigrant compound would have still happened, there was nothing he could've done to alter that, but Raine would not be in the wind with the rest of the Omega Five virus if he'd finished the job and terminated Raine.

People had died which he knew he couldn't prevent, but what about all those he'd put in danger by allowing him to escape? How would he live with that?

His stoic expression must have slipped because C asked, "Are you alright? You do realise none of this was your fault," he said.

"I beg to differ, sir. Agent Sanchez argued with me that we should not have left so soon, that we should have tried to stop Raine, but I dismissed it. I told her the mission came first and our mission was to get the data back to headquarters. If I had listened, if I had gone back, I could have prevented Raine from escaping, maybe," he replied, feeling remorse and guilt creeping through his barriers that normally held these emotions at bay.

"That's as it may be, but you did your job. If you had stayed, you could have been killed in your effort to stop Raine and then we would be without this valuable data, so you did the right thing at the time. Don't worry about Raine, I'm sure we'll catch up with him at some point. He's good but everyone makes a mistake sooner or later," C said.

"I just hope that happens before he has a chance to use the Omega Five virus again."

"Quite, well I take it from the tired expression on your face that you haven't been sitting twiddling your thumbs all this time. I take it you've been working the case from a different angle; would I be correct?" C said.

"Yes sir, I was looking into all of Raine's properties. I thought if he was going to make a run for it, we would be best prepared if we had some idea where he might run to."

"And did you, come up with somewhere I mean?"

"Considering he will know we'll be looking for him, he will choose somewhere that's not on Altair. That would be too easy to find. I think he'll go to one of his off-world places. It would have to have all the things he needs to continue his plan; I doubt he'll give it up this late in the game. He will need somewhere that has the ability to alter the virus, a facility that also has launch capabilities with enough space to house enough troops to defend it should it be discovered, and I've narrowed it down to just two."

"Show me," C said.

Chapter 25

Aria, second moon of Altair

The Coalition Defence Force commander was General Grant and after the location of the possible base was given to him, he had marshalled a strike force consisting of a contingent of the Special Forces and a starship which would transport them there. The starship would remain in orbit, controlling the skies over the moon whilst the troops invaded the base to capture or kill Raine and his men. Their primary objective though was to take control of the Omega Five virus and render it safe by destroying it.

The operation had gone as planned; the troops had been deployed as the starship had sat in geo-synchronous orbit over the base ready to protect the troops against any threat from above.

Captain Johansson led his troops down to the surface of the moon in shuttles that landed near the facility they had targeted.

Parking up and wearing combat ready Extravehicular Activity suits, they made their way across from the shuttles to the hatches where they would make ingress to the base.

"Keep alert people, we don't know what we'll be facing in there as the scans showed no activity inside," he said as he made ready to breach.

The hatches were unlocked then opened, and they entered making sure the integrity of the base was maintained until it was time when it was necessary for further action. The few soldiers who made the entrance first, spread out in the corridor beyond the airlock giving cover for those who were about to follow.

"I don't like this, sir. It appears deserted, I mean like a ghost town deserted," the young soldier by Johansson's side said, voicing the same concern as he had the moment he saw inside.

"Keep any thoughts of ghosts to yourself, soldier. Let's not spook the troops, no pun intended," he replied softly.

The moment the second group was inside he said, "Okay, let's go exploring."

It took them less than five minutes to determine that this base was, as suspected, deserted.

"Johansson to General Grant, sir they either knew we were coming or they set us up. No one's here, by my reckoning they left here hours ago sir. What are our new orders sir?"

Back at CDF HQ on Terra II, the room that had been monitoring the mission was silent. They had been watching the team move inside the base through the cameras fitted to the soldier's helmets.

"Secure the base then report back to base, Captain. Check the bases' computer logs to see if there's any indication as to where they might have gone, then get back to the ship to stand ready. Once we've analysed the data from the logs, we might have a better idea how to proceed," Grant replied.

"Copy that sir," Johansson said, then turning to his men said, "You heard the man, get everything you can from those logs and upload it to CDF HQ asap. Once we've done that, we'll seal this place up then head back to the ship."

As he watched his men work, he ruminated that someone was about to get a rocket up their ass for this cock up. He was just glad it wasn't him.

"Are you sure about this?" Sanchez asked. She was sitting next to Duncan on the flight deck of his ship just out of sensor range watching a research station in orbit around Altair.

This was the other base Duncan had shown to C after his investigation into Raine's affairs. He had chosen this one for himself and Sanchez because he thought an infiltration by just the two of them had a better chance of success than a full-frontal assault.

"It has to be," he said, hoping he sounded more confident than he felt.

Although he was acting on mission mode again, he was still having the odd feeling filter through his barriers which concerned him. He couldn't allow that to affect his efficiency, not with so much at stake.

"So, what's the plan then?" Sanchez asked.

"We create a diversion then we gain entry through the back door," he said.

Although sceptical, Sanchez said, "Okay, what exactly did you have in mind?"

"Something massive," he said with the hint of a smile.

Chapter 26

Inside the station Raine was smiling. He had outwitted them again.

He had instructed his team to continue with the altering of the virus along the specifications outlaid by the sample that had been switched by mistake. Using that as a template, more of the virus could be altered whilst it was replicated. As long as he had the Omega Five, no one dared to make a move against him.

It was the ultimate deterrent and he had it.

"How do you intend on deploying the virus?" Robbins asked. He stood next to his boss as he looked down through the safety glass windows at the lab area where the genetic altering of the virus was being completed.

Without taking his eyes off the work being done down in the lab, he said, "A team of shuttles will travel down to the immigrant sites and spray it into the air above, a bit like crop dusting back in the day."

"As soon as the shuttles start to spray, they'll know exactly where they came from. You don't think that they'll retaliate against us?" "Robbins argued. The worry he was feeling showed in his voice which Raine noticed. He turned to him, his eyes narrowing, "Are you afraid?" he asked, "because if you are, then maybe you should leave. I can't afford to have people who aren't with me one hundred per cent."

"I'm not afraid, just concerned that you might not have thought this through fully," Robbins countered.

"Of course, I've thought it through. I've planned for every eventuality and have a contingency for every outcome. I know they'll come after us when the shuttles deploy but what you failed to take into consideration is the fact they'll also know we have the Omega Five virus. They will try to barter their way out, negotiate a truce, delay my using it against them while they desperately try to come up with an end run around us. All the time they are doing that, I will be moving on to another base where we will give our mission statement."

"And what, exactly, is our mission statement?"

Raine stared at his friend, wondering how he couldn't see it, see what they were doing. After all they had done, he was still unsure.

"We are freeing our homeworld. We are showing the Coalition that they cannot play with our lives; they do not own this planet and therefore they have no say in what happens here. They cannot and will not, corrupt our planet by housing immigrants here. I will not allow them to erode our gene pool by having these immigrants mingle with our population. They are not worthy to live here. They destroyed their own world and I'm not about to allow them to do the same here. That, my friend, is our mission statement."

Nodding in agreement, Robbins said, "Okay, I'm behind you one hundred per cent, but you have to know that they'll come after us, hard after what happened with that first test."

"That was a mistake, and I agree, they will come after us but once they hear our statement and see what we can do, they'll know just how determined we are to see this through to the end. I doubt they'll have the stomach for a fight of this magnitude."

"Just as long as you know," Robbins said, "I'll go check on the progress," he added and as he was about to leave, something rocked the station with enough force it moved it from its position in high orbit sending it closer to the planet below.

"What the hell was that?" Robbins said, holding on to the wall to stop himself from being knocked to the deck.

"Something just exploded near us. That was the shockwave from the blast and it was powerful enough to move us out of position," Raine said, recognising what had happened. Into his com link, he called the bridge, "Get us back under control now and move us back into position," he screamed at them. The sensation of movement was unnerving as he knew there was only one way this entire station could move after a jolt like that and that was down toward the planet below.

He looked at Robbins, his eyes going wide in disbelief. Although this shouldn't be happening, he knew exactly what it was.

"They're here," he said.

Chapter 27

Duncan had the AI move the ship forward close to the station but under cover of the stealth cloak. Once they were in position, he instructed it to leave a space mine behind.

As soon as that was accomplished, they moved to the opposite side of the station and waited. The mine was set to explode five minutes after they left it so they made preparations while they waited.

Donning their EVA battle suits complete with a full armoury package, they were ready to go.

"Do you think this will work?" Sanchez asked, some of her nervousness adding a slight tremble into her voice.

"I'm eighty-five per cent sure, or maybe seventy-five per cent."

"Do you always have to be so accurate? I'd prefer it if you'd just said you were pretty sure and left it at that."

"If you must know, since we've been working together, I haven't been as focussed as I usually am. You distract me and I find it disconcerting."

"Oh, so now it's my fault, is it?" she snapped back angrily.

"Yes, I never wanted a partner, never needed one before and I told C it was a mistake."

"Why am I a distraction do you think?" she asked a little calmer now. She was still angry, but she knew there was something more going on here. "I tell you what, if we ever get out of this in one piece you can answer that question then. Right now, we have a job to do so why don't we just do it," she said, not giving him chance to respond.

Duncan was relieved in a way, as he didn't want to talk about what he thought the reason for his distraction was, at least not now when they had this mission to complete. He needed to stay focussed so he concentrated on blocking everything else from his mind and said, "Yes, let's do this."

The mine exploded sending out a shockwave that ploughed into the station knocking it off its orbit.

"Right, go," Duncan said, and they exited their ship through the hatch. Powering their thruster packs sent them zipping across the space between them and the station.

With all the attention fixed firmly on the cause of the explosion, no one would be looking at the opposite side.

They quickly reached the station in no time at all and found the hatch they needed. Duncan had the door open by entering a universal unlock code once more and they were inside.

Keeping their suits on, they entered the station through the airlock and began their search for the virus. Their primary objective was to locate the virus then destroy it. Locating Raine was a secondary objective and could be handled once the virus had been dealt with.

"Any ideas where the safest place to store the virus will be, if it's not in a lab?" Sanchez asked as they looked around.

"The lab, it has to be there, it's the only area on this station that has the capability to contain it safely," Duncan replied.

Sanchez was looking through the station's itinerary on a screen on the wall.

"I think I found it, deck twelve. That entire deck is taken up with medical labs and research areas. If he has the virus anywhere, my guess is it'll be there," she said.

"Good work," he said as he looked around for a turbo lift.

"Over there, we can use that and descend down to that deck and do what we came for," he said.

They ran over to it and got in, selecting deck twelve from the controls. The descent was fast and they were there in a few seconds. As they entered the deck, they looked for the lab areas, which they found straight away. They were on a walkway that had a wall of glass that overlooked a dropped area where a variety of tests were being run on something they couldn't quite make out from this angle.

"We need to get in there," Sanchez said, but Duncan was already moving toward the door. The room beyond was a clean room, everyone inside wore the same white garments that covered their entire body, including their heads. Transparent face shields allowed them to see what they were doing with a variety of lenses attached for extreme close-up work.

Hands and feet were covered so that nothing could contaminate what they were working on through touch.

As Duncan entered, they all turned to see who it was and then as they saw the weapon in his hand, they all froze on the spot.

"Show me the Omega Five," he ordered.

No one moved at first until Duncan aimed his Walther deliberately at one of them, his pretence of being ready to shoot galvanised them into motion.

"It's over there, in that container," the person being targeted blurted out, pointing vigorously in the direction he mentioned, desperate to get him to move his gun away from him.

Sanchez moved over to the container that had been indicated and looked inside through the clear glass top. It was another clear container, long and cylindrical sealed at both ends but with adaptors at each end for a probe to be inserted to either remove a sample or add something to it.

"I think this is it," she said, a little triumphantly.

Pointing his Walther at the person in charge, Duncan said, "Omega Five just like any other virus can be destroyed by intense heat, right?"

"Yes, that's correct," replied the man, a little concerned as to what they were going to do.

"What temperature do we need to kill that sample?" Duncan asked, keeping his gun trained on him but also watching the others in case they suddenly grew a set of balls and considered taking him on.

"At least one hundred degrees Celsius for a minute will do it. Anything lower than that and the time needed to kill it entirely would have to be increased."

"Is that all of it?" Duncan asked.

"That's all of it here, yes."

"Okay, move out people, get to a safe location because it's going to get real hot in here real soon," Duncan said. He walked over to Sanchez and said, "Get them moving out of here."

"Won't that alert Raine to where we are?" she argued.

"By the time they learn that, it'll be too late to save the virus. After that, we get the hell out of here," Duncan replied. He wasn't looking at her, his attention was on getting the virus container out of the cabinet.

"You heard the man, get moving," she said to the others brandishing her gun at them.

What was about to happen suddenly dawned on them, and they all ran for the exits. Sanchez turned back to Duncan once the room was clear to watch what he was doing.

He had placed the tube containing the virus on top of the cabinet and was positioning several incendiary grenades around it, pinning it upright and in place.

He looked at his handiwork then took a step back.

"All we need do now is set the timer and get the hell out of here," he said.

"Do it then, because I've a feeling we're about to have some company real soon," she said.

He leant forward and primed each grenade, ten in all then backed off.

"Okay let's go," he said and ran for the door. As he went through it, the room behind him erupted in several explosions that were white hot from the phosphorus in the grenades. The blasts took out the walls in a fiery display that burned hotter than hell itself, or so it seemed.

Duncan and Sanchez were knocked over by the blast, but they got up as fast as they could and sprinted away from the spreading flames that had engulfed the entire lab area. Duncan had placed his grenades as close to the gas pipes the lab used to power the burners. When they had exploded, they had ignited that too, adding to the intensity of the blast, increasing the heat factor and destroying the entire lab.

Flames burst out from the pipes leading to the container for the gas igniting that too. The inside of the lab was engulfed in a fire so hot the walls began to melt. Unable to contain the conflagration any longer, the fire burst from the confines of the lab to spread through corridors, up walls and elevator shafts seeking new ground to burn.

"If they didn't know we were here before, they sure as hell know now," Sanchez said as they ran for their lives toward the exit.

Chapter 28

Sanchez was right, on the bridge the explosion was felt just after the station had regained its orbit position.

"Shit, they got to it," Raine said, but he didn't show any signs of concern, which confused Robbins.

"Why are you looking at me like that?" he asked when he saw the confusion causing furrows across Robbins' forehead.

"Why are you not angry, why didn't you allow me to go down there if you knew what they were after?" Robbins asked.

"Because I expected them and already planned for it. Don't worry, they may have destroyed the sample in the lab, which is what I hoped they'd go for. Now maybe they'll leave us alone for a bit."

"I'm not with you, what do you mean?" Robbins asked.

"I already offloaded more of the Omega Five virus to another base. I knew they'd come after it wherever we went so I allowed them to find us and make their play to destroy it, which they did. Now judging by the explosion, we just felt, and by what the internal sensors are telling us, they destroyed the entire lab and probably hoped the rest of this station will be destroyed along with it. That's okay too because we can then go off on our way without them knowing, probably thinking we're all dead."

Robbins smiled as it was all laid out for him. It was genius really and yet so simple.

"Wow," he said, unable to think of anything else to say.

"Get ready to evacuate, we'll give them what they want," Raine said gleefully. His plan was finally working out as he'd foreseen it.

Duncan and Sanchez reached the hatch they had entered through in less time it had taken to reach the lab. All the time they had been running away the effects of what they had done were evident throughout the station.

Warning alarms sounded informing staff to use the escape pods as explosions from the fire they had started rent through the lower decks destroying everything in their path.

What escape pods could be accessed were used by the staff of the station and viewed from outside it appeared as if a swarm of hornets had left the station. Getting to the hatch had not been easy as they had to avoid the escaping crew members as they fled in their panic fuelled haste. Once they reached the hatch though, Duncan hoped there would be no more obstacles to overcome.

Duncan urged Sanchez through the hatch into space and fired his thruster pack to put some distance between them and the station. Glancing behind him as they were moving away, he saw the explosions ripping through the station. It was quite the spectacle but he knew it came with some cost. Innocent lives were lost inside the station, those who didn't make it to safety in time, but he weighed those against the vast number he had saved by destroying the remainder of the Omega Five virus. Any loss of life was tragic and should be avoided at all costs, but there were those times when some lives had to be sacrificed in order to save others. This was one of those times. He felt some guilt over the fact that those who died here today were not given the chance or choice whether to sacrifice themselves. That choice was taken from them. It was a small amount of guilt that would no doubt grow as soon as his barriers came down.

"Ship, come and pick us up quick. That station is about to blow," he said.

In front of him, no farther than a few metres his ship appeared as the stealth cloak was dropped.

"I am here, Commander, I have followed my orders and monitored your progress throughout and anticipated you would need an earlier ex-fil," the AI responded.

The hatch opened in the side and the two of them entered quickly. Duncan kept watch on the station behind them, mentally calculating how long they had left before the inevitable destruction blew it to smithereens.

"Get us moving, Ship, now," he said forcefully as they closed the hatch behind them. They were still in the airlock as the ship boosted the engines up to full burn thrusting them away from the station just in time as a massive explosion tore it apart sending a shockwave out to chase them.

Fiery debris that soon burned out in the vacuum of space was scattered through the ether. The shockwave was in a race to catch the ship but it lost its momentum at the last moment, allowing the ship to escape.

"That was close," observed Sanchez as the two of them climbed out of the airlock, a little shaken by the sudden increase in speed. The inertia dampeners had saved them from being turned into strawberry jam on the walls of the airlock, the physics of which had always baffled Duncan. He was just grateful it worked otherwise the speeds required for interstellar travel would be impossible to survive.

Getting his breathing back to normal, Duncan said, "Okay, Ship, take us back to headquarters."

He began walking toward the bridge when Sanchez said, "Seeing as how this mission is over, all bar the writing up of reports and the inevitable debriefs, how about you answer my question."

Without looking at her, he said, "Which was?"

"Why am I such a distraction to you?"

Before Duncan could reply, the ship's AI said, "Commander, according to mission protocols I began running sensor scans of the debris field before we left. I found something, sir."

"Saved by the bell once again," Sanchez told him.

"We're on our way," Duncan said, increasing his speed from a walk to a fast jog. He had the feeling that this wasn't over just yet and he was about to be proven right.

Chapter 29

"Okay Ship, show me what you got," Duncan said as the two agents reached the bridge.

Dropping down into the pilot's seat, and Sanchez into the seat next to him, a screen appeared in front which began showing the station being destroyed.

"Commander I ran scans on the station as it was destroyed and I found some anomalous readings," the AI reported.

Duncan was watching the screen as the image of the explosion was slowed down so every detail could be scrutinised.

"What are we seeing here?" Sanchez asked, leaning forward to see a little better.

"The scans showed a faint energy trace leaving the station just before the final explosion. The signal was obscured by the energy being blasted out from the explosion so if you weren't looking for it, the chances are it would have been missed."

"Any idea what that signature could belong to?" Duncan asked.

"A ship, sir. I believe they used the explosion to cover their departure."

Duncan stared at the screen watching the trace signal, once it had been highlighted by the AI, it was easier to see. He watched as it left the station as the explosion expanded and then entered a hyperspace window and was gone.

"Shit!" he muttered in an uncharacteristic display of anger.

"What now?" Sanchez asked.

"Now we start all over again. Raine was a step ahead of us again, he knew we would find both bases and he was ready for us. He had his escape plan all ready to go for when someone came for him."

"How could he know we'd use fire to destroy the virus though, surely that was something that he couldn't plan ahead for," Sanchez argued.

"How else would you destroy a virus, fire is, and always will be the easiest, most efficient way to kill one. Omega Five is no different in that respect. Raine has proven he's an expert tactician, so it's not too hard to think that he would have a contingency in place for an attempt to invade the station. He would adapt any plan he had for any given circumstance. It's one of the things they teach in the Special Forces."

"What about the virus though, at least we destroyed that," Sanchez said.

"Did we though? He certainly had enough time to replicate enough of it to use elsewhere. If he had expected an attempt to destroy it, he would certainly leave enough of it around for us to think we had accomplished the mission. He probably thinks we have left there thinking we did it, and there is no longer any reason to look for him. He probably thinks we thought he died in the explosion leaving him free to do whatever he wants to any time scale he deems appropriate as there is no pressure to find him or the virus anymore. That is his first mistake and our best advantage."

"How is that to our advantage?"

"Because he now thinks he's invisible, no one is looking to find him and he'll get sloppy, make more mistakes. This time though we'll be ready."

"I hope you're right," Sanchez said.

"So do I," he replied.

Sanchez put a hand on his arm and looked at him. "I'm not interested why you feel I'm a distraction to you, Duncan. That doesn't matter at the moment, it's not important. What is important though is that we find Raine and stop him from using that virus again. For that, we need the old Duncan Pryde. I need you to put whatever it is that's distracting you out of your mind so you can focus on this mission. Can you do that?" she said.

If he was being totally honest with himself, he would have to answer that he didn't know, instead he said, "I can do that, yes," because it was what she needed to hear.

"When we get to headquarters, Ship, put us down in the usual spot but stand ready for a fast departure," he said.

"Copy that, Commander."

Duncan felt some of his old resolve returning, the same self-control he prided himself on having. It made him able to stand apart from others, to perform his job better than others because he faced no emotional ties, no emotional barriers to overcome. Nothing held him back from making the tough decisions, and therefore he got the job done faster than most.

He had to keep that now if he wanted to end this with Raine. He had to stop him from doing the unthinkable because it wouldn't end there. It was just a step in the wrong direction, one once he'd taken could never be turned around from. It would be a path that would shape the rest of his life.

He didn't care about that, what he cared about were all the lives he would end once he set foot on that path.

By the time they reached Terra II, his jaw was set in determination, his eyes cold and hard as they focussed on one thing only, ending Marcus Raine's run of terror.

Chapter 30

Altair

"Why did you bring us back here?" Robbins asked when he saw where the second jump had brought them. The first hyperspace jump took them out to the edge of the star system which was followed quickly by the second which brought them straight back to their homeworld.

"Because, my friend, it is probably the last place they would look for us, if they are looking at all that is," Raine told him. "Look, as far as they are concerned, we all died in that station when it blew up, so they think it's all over. Why look for us at all, right? If they do discover we escaped death, then they'll probably think we made a run for it as far away from here as possible, so here is the last place they'll look, right?" he added.

"So, we're going to carry on with the mission, right?" Robbins asked.

Raine blew his cheeks out, "Of course," he said, "why wouldn't we, like I said, no one is looking for us."

"Well, when you kill all the immigrants on Altair don't you think that they just might put two and two together?

"They'd be stupid not to. You know, I'd love to see their faces when they realise what fools I made them out to be."

"You're missing the point here, Marcus. When that happens, they will come for us, you know that, right?"

"Stop stressing, I've been three steps ahead of those idiots all the way through this, you don't think I have a plan for that as well?"

"For God's sake man, I hope so, 'cause I don't feel like dying just yet, no matter how important you think this cause is. I'm just in this for the money."

Raine looked at him, his eyes travelled up and down him as his mouth turned down in the corners in disgust. "What money, I haven't asked for any money and I'm not about to," he said.

"But you will, right? I mean you have the virus; you know they'll come for us eventually so what better way to stop them than to threaten them with it. Say you'll use it if they don't pay you enough. Or auction it off, I'm sure some warlord or crime lord somewhere in the galaxy would love to get their hands on this thing. Why not auction it off to the highest bidder?"

"Are you insane, I'm not in this for the money. I'm making a point and protecting my home at the same time. I will use the Omega Five to ensure this planet is treated fairly and not considered a dumping ground for the galaxy's refuse or discard."

"Why not get rich at the same time though?" Robbins continued to argue.

"I'm already rich, and besides, the threat alone is enough."

"You may be rich, but what about the rest of us? We followed you into this not because we believed in the cause but we saw a chance of becoming richer than our wildest dreams."

This was something he hadn't foreseen, he'd always assumed that his followers were true believers, like himself. He wasn't that naïve that he thought they were all the same, there would be a few who had their own reasons for joining him, whether it was some sadistic relief to see others punished or simply hurt or some other reason, it didn't matter. But to find his right-hand man, his friend, was only helping to get rich was shocking to him. He thought he knew him better than that, which was clearly not the case.

"Okay, I take your point and will address it when we're done. I will ensure you all get what's coming to you, that's a promise," he said. It was a promise he would keep because betrayal was something he would never tolerate, so in voicing his reasons for being there, Robbins had signed his own death warrant.

"Now let's put this behind us and get back to work, there's still so much to be done," he said with a cruel smile. His path was now clearer than ever, and it was a path that didn't include his friend anymore.

Chapter 31

MI7 HQ, Terra II

"Congratulations on the success of your mission you two," C said as they entered his office.

"Hold on to the congratulations for a little longer, sir. I don't think this is over just yet," Duncan corrected him.

He saw his boss's face darken; his smile of relief slowly turned into a scowl of disappointment.

"What exactly do you mean by that, Agent Pryde?" he asked.

"My ship ran scans of the station as it exploded and picked up an energy signature that we think was from an escaping ship. Under closer scrutiny we saw it enter a hyperspace window leaving the star system. That could only have occurred if it was what we thought, a ship. Sir, I think it safe to say that Raine is still at large and if he went to the trouble of planning an escape in advance then it's also safe to assume he has more of the Omega Five virus with him," Duncan explained.

"Well that just ruined my day," C said, leaning back in his chair.

"We have one advantage working in our favour sir," Duncan offered.

"Which is what, because at the moment I'm not seeing too many positives here?" C asked.

"He thinks he got away clean with this, so his security won't be as good as it has been. He won't be expecting anyone looking for him which gives us the opportunity to find him."

"How might I ask, will we be able to do that, he could be anywhere by now?" C countered.

Duncan smiled a half smile.

"Using what we already know about him and his motives for his initial plan, I think I know where he is, sir," he said.

Chapter 32

Altair

The underground base was exactly what Raine needed for his operation. It was an old abandoned Military base used by the Altairan forces to train them for induction into the CDF.

Now, it was just a shell but since Raine had envisioned his plan, he had taken precautions for every eventuality he could foresee, one of which was the need to retreat into this base. This meant he had to ensure the base was ready. He had work crews working through the night before he made his first move just so this place would be ready in case it was needed.

He oversaw the transport of the virus in safe containers to their new home in the lab where they would be genetically altered under the supervision of his medical scientist staff. They knew what needed to be done and he would make sure it was done.

The base had a large open space in the centre of the main hangar, which was where they parked the ship. To gain entry to this, there was a tunnel angled upward, basically a runway angled up at forty-five degrees with a huge door at the end that opened to allow ships in or out. Around his hangar were tunnels leading off into the other areas of the base, like spokes on a wheel. At the moment, the most important area was the lab which Raine had made sure was ready for their arrival.

Personnel quarters were in another section. The remaining tunnels had various other functions and were left unused for the moment.

The base was hidden out in the open wastelands near the planet's equator. It was an area that was never visited and, in that respect, the perfect location for a secret military base.

Raine sat in his office away from the rest of his men needing the time to think. He knew Robbins was not sold on this operation, not truly as he was so that being said, how many of the rest of them had he infected with his profit-based motives he wondered.

Tapping into the Interweb, he searched through local info pages on the news websites to see what was being reported about the immigration problem. He already knew there was a faction in the public who thought the same as him about not allowing those from off world to be dumped here so he searched for more of them. He knew of a few groups around that had the same politics as him especially regarding this issue and had made contact with some of them. What he needed now were some of them who were more militant about their views and who would act aggressively if required to.

He soon found what he needed and reached out to them through a secure com link.

Phillip Kaufman took the call at his group's headquarters.

He was a bear of a man, standing six feet three with an enormous barrel chest. His head was round like a bowling ball and just as smooth. It sat atop a thick neck attached to broad shoulders that had a solid torso beneath. Thickly muscled arms and legs gave the impression of immense strength which was made even more threatening by his steely gaze. One look from those dark, almost black eyes had reduced many men to quivering wrecks before.

After serving with honour in his planet's military, he had resigned his commission when they had wanted him to join the CDF and fight for them as many of his countrymen had done. He had refused on the grounds that he didn't mind fighting to keep his homeworld safe but why should he fight other people's? Other people's fight had nothing whatsoever to do with him, so he resigned, leaving a glittering career in tatters. A story was quickly circulated that he was afraid to fight, and he was a coward.

This harmed not only his career, but his reputation also. When he learned it had been started by one of the soldiers under him who had agreed to join the CDF, he sought him out in the attempt to show him the error of his ways and to ask him to recant the rumour.

It didn't go so well and he lost his temper when he refused, so he killed him. He broke the man's neck after a quickly fought scuffle which there was only ever going to be one outcome.

Now a wanted man, Kaufman went underground going off the grid. A small group of his fellow soldiers who agreed with his decision supported him and went with him to form a militia that quickly grew in numbers until they were over a thousand strong with more joining on a regular basis.

Using the Wastelands as a base, Kaufman and his group became a rising voice against the policies of the present government and grew support from more of the public after they agreed to house the immigrants from the dying world.

This was the thing that Kaufman had said was wrong in his joining to fight other people's battles. Now the government had brought other people's troubles and placed them firmly on their own doorstep.

When he spoke, people began to listen, especially when he advocated for another world to be found for the immigrants. Let them make their new start on another new world. They weren't wanted here, nor were they needed.

He found a comrade in Raine when he learned they shared the same viewpoint and when Raine called him, he was more than happy to take the call.

The news medias around the world had already started to paint him as a terrorist, so Kaufman knew that they would get along. If the media were calling him names, then it was to divert attention from what he was fighting against.

"Mister Raine, what do I owe the pleasure of this call?" he said, noting they were on a secure channel, he was taking no chances. They really were out to get him then.

"I would like a moment of your time which could prove to be very rewarding for both of us," Raine said.

"Go ahead, I'm listening," Kaufman replied.

"You may have heard I am being hailed as a terrorist after the deaths of those immigrants at the induction centre, some of which is true."

"Which part?"

"I am responsible for the deaths of those immigrants, but I am no terrorist, I am a patriot."

"What is it you want from me?"

"I have at my disposal the means of being able to wipe out every last immigrant on this planet and in doing so, send a message to the government, indeed the Coalition itself, that we will not be inundated with vermin. We will not tolerate having the galaxy's scum and degenerates dropped on our world. In short it will say, leave us be, we are fine as we are."

There was a lengthy pause while Kaufman thought through what he'd been told.

Finally, he said, "And you think this message will prevent any retaliation coming your way?"

"It will certainly make them think twice and if they decide to act, I will still have the means to level their homeworlds and kill millions of their own. When they learn this, they will surely not risk moving against me."

"What is it you want from me? You called me not because you wanted to chat, but because you want something," Kaufman said.

"It has come to my attention that certain members of my organisation have altered their perspective over what I intend on doing. I am not fully sure if I can trust them anymore so I am asking you to watch my back."

"What makes you think you can trust me?"

"I have read your record and heard what you have said. We share the same view over these damned immigrants. I want them gone as do you so why not help each other to finally get rid of them?"

There was another pause which Raine had expected. What he was asking was not to be considered lightly. It needed thought and deep consideration before replying in any way. Just as he was about to check to see if the call had been terminated, he heard Kaufman say, "When do you want me to start?"

Chapter 33

MI7 HQ Terra II

"Before I can sanction this operation, I have to be sure you have got it right. I can't afford to send in the troops on just a hunch, you understand that right?" C said.

"Perfectly sir. Why not allow Sanchez and I to return to Altair to see what we can learn? When we have enough on Raine and what he plans going forward I will let you know," Duncan offered.

"I'll allow that only if you promise to give a sitrep every hour. If you miss one check in, I'll pull the plug and send in the troops, is that understood?"

"Perfectly sir," Duncan agreed.

"Use your cover as a consultant for UniTrav. and check out what you can find about Raine. Find out if he's still alive and where he might be. When you get eyes on him, call it in and I'll pass it on to the CDF who are eager to take him down."

"What if there's no time to wait for them to arrive sir?"

"Then you'll have to take whatever action is necessary to prevent that from happening."

"Copy that sir," Duncan said and got up to leave and Sanchez followed his lead.

At the door C said, "Take care, you two, no unnecessary risks. Is that clear?"

"Perfectly sir," Sanchez said.

"Copy that sir," Duncan added.

"Now, go on then and remember, hourly check ins," C said.

Duncan waved affirmation as he closed the door behind them.

"Where are you off to again, Duncan?" Goodchild asked as she saw the two of them emerge from the boss's office.

"Back to Altair to check on a few things," he replied.

"I thought you'd finished it all off and the case was closed," she said looking from him to Sanchez wondering what had happened.

"Seems we might have missed something," he said.

"It's not like you to miss something, whatever could it be?" Goodchild said smiling.

"We think Raine is still alive," he said.

This hit Goodchild like a jolt of electricity. "Christ, and you're going back to finish off the job?"

"We have to confirm he's alive first so this op is just a fishing expedition. Keep tabs on us though, just in case we find some trouble," he said.

"Always," Goodchild replied, placing her hand on his arm then removing it quickly as she caught Sanchez watching her.

The two agents moved off then heading for the landing pad and their ship.

Duncan said, "Ship, fire up the engines. We're going back to Altair."

"Ready and waiting for your arrival, Commander," the AI replied.

"She's into you, you know," Sanchez said once they were out of Goodchild's earshot.

"What are you talking about?" he asked, truly having no idea what she meant.

"Goodchild, she's into you."

"Don't be ridiculous," he snapped back a little too fast for comfort.

"I think M'lud doth protest too much," she said in a mock English aristocratic accent.

"You really are annoying; you know that right?" he said.

"Nice one, divert attention away from the point of the discussion. Is that because you're also into her perhaps, but you'd rather not say?"

"Where is this coming from?" he asked.

"You didn't answer my question."

"Look, we have a job to do, so let's just focus on that shall we?"

"Yes sir, Commander sir," she replied, giving him a mock salute.

"And they wonder why I prefer to work alone," he muttered to himself.

Chapter 34

Altair

As the ship re-entered normal space close to Altair, Duncan said, "Ship, put us down at the nearest city to the Wastelands."

"Copy that, Commander," the AI replied and steered toward the planet already having chosen which space port to use.

"The Wastelands, why there?" Sanchez asked. They had travelled in silence since leaving Terra II which had pleased Duncan no end. Her incessant rattling was wearing thin and he had to concentrate even harder than ever to prevent it from getting to him.

"If Raine is here, he's already got a base set up and where better to hide it than out there. No one ever goes there, it's just miles of desert. The military used to have training bases out here away from the population, but there was push back from the government when the Coalition ordered the Altairan government to send some of their men to join the

CDF. It was supposed to unite the planets in the COP, give them a combined sense of purpose but some of the soldiers here thought differently about it. They deemed they were being stripped of their individuality, their sense of patriotism, and so there was a minor revolt and in the end, the government shut it down."

"I heard about that, but I thought it was just a rumour, you know, an urban legend thing."

"No, it actually happened. It forced the CDF to make induction a purely voluntary thing from then on."

"I understand that, but why close down the base?"

"To draw a line under the whole incident. The government was eager to appear as if they were doing something on behalf of their population, so closing down the base was seen to be closing off the incident. Other bases were still used, but they chose to close that particular one as a symbol that this whole incident was finished. It backfired though because it then appeared as if the government was brushing the incident under the carpet, hiding it away as if in shame. It turned out to be one of those no-win situations for them, no matter what they did, someone would think it was the wrong decision."

"So, you're thinking that Raine is using the abandoned base now."

"It's a theory I've been considering, but how to get there without being noticed is going to be difficult, and that's just the first hurdle we'll have to get over. How to get inside will be a massive task."

"First things first, if he is using the base, someone is going to know about it. If it was abandoned as you say, then he would have to make it fit for his use before moving in, right? Someone would have done that work. We find them and we have proof that he's using it."

"He's likely covered his tracks over that, probably used people loyal to him or separate contractors who had no contact with the owner. It would take too long to work through all the people involved."

"Okay, how about this then. He would probably reach out to others who shared the same views as him to form a sort of para-military set-up for when he makes his move. He'll need protection when the shit hits the fan so what about looking into various groups who have the same views as him? We could probably keep tabs on them to see what they're doing."

"Commander, I have that list of paramilitary groups you requested, I've downloaded it to both your PINs," the AI said.

Sanchez's jaw dropped open a little as she said, "You already thought of that."

"Yes, it seemed fairly obvious he would reach out to others who shared similar political views over the influx of refugees and among those he would more than likely gravitate towards those who have a military background such as himself. I asked the Ship to search for them as we came in to land on Terra II."

"What the hell do you need me for then?" she said, immediately regretting it.

"My point exactly. I already said I work best alone and that you would be, are a distraction."

"Here we go again with the distraction, which you never addressed by the way."

"You said not to, remember?"

"I did, I must admit to that. So why don't we agree on finishing this mission, I'll try not to get in your way so you can do your thing and once we're done, we're done. You will never have to put up with me ever again, deal?"

"Deal," he agreed much too easily for her taste and so she turned away from him. He should have felt relief, if he felt anything, but he didn't. Although it seemed he'd won and was going to get his way, it didn't seem that much of a victory. Why was it so important to work alone anyway? Why was he even having these thoughts, these doubts? Normally his mind was clear with one singular focus but just lately he had all these other thoughts milling around in his head distracting him from his objective and he was not used to it. He didn't know how to deal with it.

In the past, he would close down his mind and do the job, then once it was over his barriers would come down and he would relax and enjoy what time off he was granted. He had a close circle of friends who knew nothing about what he did for a living and that was how he liked it. Now, he was part- nered with a beautiful woman who drove him mad. Invading his thoughts, constantly questioning him on his decisions, wanting to know about him, what his life was like, why? Why would she want to know, why couldn't he block her from his mind?

"Shit!" he said before realising he said it.

"Excuse me?" she asked.

"Nothing," he replied, concentrating on landing the ship, even though the AI did all the work.

With a shrug of her shoulders, she looked away again and he relaxed again.

He'd realised why he was feeling like this and how much of a jackass he was for not realising it sooner.

Knowing this made his job so much harder.

Chapter 35

Having parked the ship at the space port they took the Nimbus into the city. Through the AI Duncan had searched through the list of hotels available and had chosen one. When they arrived, they parked in front of the gleaming edifice that was the Grand Hotel. One hundred and fifty-five floors of luxury apartment, suites and rooms. Duncan had booked a suite that had two separate bedrooms.

It wasn't chosen to impress Sanchez but to facilitate their working together without running to and from separate rooms which might arouse suspicion.

As soon as they got out of the car, magnetic clamps came up out of the road and attached to the sides of the car then the entire slab of road it was sitting on descended below ground to be replaced by another slab covering the hole left there. Once below ground the car was taken down into the parking area on a rail system that travelled along until it reached an empty space. Once this journey ended the slab along with the car tilted up onto its side, the car held securely in place by the magnetic clamps, and then slotted into a space in between several other cars. In this way the space used for the car parking was utilised in a more efficient manner allowing more vehicles to be parked than if they remained upright on its wheels.

Booking in to the hotel was as easy as showing his forearm to the scanner near the door. The chip imbedded in his arm gave all the relevant details required to identify him including the cover identity he was using, Robert Banks, a consultant with UniTrav. Sanchez followed suit following him through into the lobby and on to the bank of elevators that would take them to their suite. Entry into the rooms was achieved once booking had been completed. The entry code was input into the visitor's ID chip so that they could access the room by swiping their arm across the door sensor. This cut out the need for key cards which had to be re-used and re-coded every time and also could be mislaid. This negated the need of all of that and made checking in and out much easier and faster. Once a client had booked out the ID chip was updated and all hotel data removed from the visitor's chip.

"Nice, glad I'm not the one paying for this," Sanchez said as she entered the main lounge of the suite.

White leather furniture sat on top of the lush carpeting throughout the main lounge that also doubled as dining room should the guest decided to eat in. It could just as easily be used as an office should the guest require that too. Bedrooms were at either end to the main lounge area which was on two levels. Three steps led up from the sitting area where a three-seater leather sofa and two comfortable armchairs sat opposite a glass topped coffee table. The steps led up to the dining/office area where a table of polished oak sat in front of floor to ceiling windows that gave a marvellous view of the city below.

Each bedroom was fitted with a king size bed, white fitted wardrobes and en-suite facilities. It was the most luxurious thing Sanchez had ever seen.

"This place is amazing," she said her eyes wide open in surprise as she looked around. Finally, she threw herself down on the sofa stretching out her hands behind her head smiling broadly.

"We're here to work, remember?" Duncan chided her.

"Of course," she said, "what do you want me to do?"

She had an inviting look in her eyes which he tried to ignore then said, "We need to see who Raine has been in contact with."

"How do you do that if we don't know where he is or even if he's alive?"

"We check to see if there's been any significant movement among the militia groups, he was likely to contact. If they are doing anything unusual then we follow them and see what they're up to."

"Copy that Boss," she said springing up off the sofa.

She went over to the dining table and took out her PIN and placed it on the table. In seconds she had a link to the Interweb and started to searches for the militias that they were looking for.

"I think I may have found something Boss," she said.

"What's with this 'Boss' thing?" Duncan asked. It almost seemed she went out of her way to be a distraction despite telling him to do his job.

"Sorry Boss, won't happen again," she said with a mischievous smile.

Sighing, Duncan moved over to see what she had found, "Show me what you found," he said.

"I think this guy fits the bill, wouldn't you?" she said showing him the page she had found, "and he's on the move."

Chapter 36

K aufman sat in the front seat of the jet copter as it took off. There was a group of his men in the passenger section with more in the two other copters which formed this convoy.

They were heading out to rendezvous with Raine at a predestined location. He knew Raine was playing it safe and that's why he hadn't given him the real location of his new base. It was a test to see if he could be trusted. It was okay though because it's something he would've done had circumstances been reversed.

He was wearing a headset so he could communicate with the pilot and the rest of the men inside the chopper. Through all the years of engineering making choppers more efficient, fast or more manoeuvrable one thing always remained the same. The noise inside the vehicle was excruciatingly loud and headsets had to be worn to communicate otherwise the sound would drown out any voice no matter how loud you shouted.

"Do you trust this guy?" Johnathan Tate asked. At the moment he was flying the aircraft and was Kaufman's second in command. They had served together in the Special Forces and he had followed his friend when he resigned his commission to follow him. He was a large man with a shock of unruly red hair as tall as Kaufman.

"I'm not sure yet. He certainly seems legit but I'll know more when I meet him face to face. I'll know if he's full of shit when I can look him in the eye when he speaks to me," Kaufman replied.

"Didn't he say he was responsible for the attack on the immigrant induction centre? I thought it was an accident. Some people were saying the immigrants brought a disease with them others said it was some militia who attacked them. Are you saying it was him, but how did he do it?"

"I'm not saying it, he is. He didn't give any details but let's face it, if he has something that can cause what happened there then I'd rather be on his good side than opposing him. It's a matter of survival, and I plan to survive."

"I hear you, and take your point."

"I take your point about how he could be full of shit but this is the best way to test that theory. If it turns out to be true then we just go back the way we came, but if he's legit, then I for one want to be on the winning side in this thing, don't you?"

"You got that right, winning side all the way."

Flipping a switch on the comms he was able to talk to the rest of the men as well, he said, "Whatever happens down there I want you all to be on the alert. Treat this as a mission where we are going into a possible hostile situation. I want covers the moment we set down with snipers getting into position to cover us all and acting as overwatch. Stay frosty because we just don't know for sure what we'll be facing so I want us all to be ready."

When that was done, he said to the pilot, "Okay, we're here, take us down."

"This is boring," Sanchez said. They had remained inactive now for an hour or two and it was getting to her.

"This is the job, ninety-nine per cent of the time it's sitting around waiting for something to happen and the remaining one per cent in sheer terror because of the action. It's what we signed up for and if you can't hack it then you should find another line of work," he replied. Duncan was sitting in one of the arm chairs relaxing. He had detached a part of his mind so he was removed from the mission just waiting for the results which he knew was coming.

Sanchez though, was pacing the room like the caged tigress she was. He could tell she was itching to get into combat, her time would come, he knew well enough about that. It would just take time; she would just have to learn to cope with the down time better.

"Why don't you check to see where that militia is?" he said to give her something to do.

"You're just giving me something to do to alleviate my boredom, aren't you?" she said seeing through his ruse.

"What if I am, we still need to see what he's up to, don't we? You did say he looks to be the best candidate so far."

"Okay, I'll check," she agreed moving to the office are to check her PIN once more. She had located the subject on the Interweb and then placed a tag on him so his location would be flagged. When she checked her PIN, the tag was stationary.

"Wherever he went, he stopped now," she said staring at the small screen of her device.

"Stopped, stopped where?" he asked.

"It looks like he's somewhere in the Wastelands."

"I wonder what he's doing out there?" he said.

Kaufman stood outside the chopper looking around for any sign of Raine.

"If that rat bastard is a no show, I swear to God I'm gonna hunt him down and kill the sonofabitch," he thought.

"Tell your men to get back into the choppers," a voice said from off to his right. He spun to look but there was no sign of anyone.

"Do it right now or I'm gone," Raine said.

"Hey, you called me, remember?" Kaufman replied angrily, "Show yourself or I'm outta here," he demanded.

From close to his left Raine rose up from a prone position on the ground. He was wearing a camouflage suit which enabled him to blend in with the background.

"Nice," observed Kaufman as Raine stood up, he had a pistol aimed right at his head.

"Tell your men to get back on board the choppers, now," he said and Kaufman gave a hand signal for them to comply.

Once they were alone on the sand Raine indicated for Kaufman to follow him farther away as he wanted to talk in private.

"Well, Raine, I'm here, what is it you wanted to say?" Kaufman said.

"What would you say to having all the immigrants removed from our world, and in a way that the Coalition will never try the same thing again?" Raine said.

"You know the answer to that already. I'm of the same view as you are over this matter."

"Good, then here's what I want you to do."

Chapter 37

"It seems like your suspect is on the move again," Sanchez said as she watched the screen.

"Let me know where they end up. See if you can get an exact fix on them then we can decide what to do next," Duncan replied.

"It seems he's moving to another part of the Wastelands."

"That must be where his base is."

"Makes sense for a militia to stay away from the city."

"Let me know the moment his tag stops, that'll be where his base will be."

"Copy that," Sanchez said and Duncan was waiting for her snarky comment but this time she was all business.

A few minutes later she said, "Okay, I have his location."

"Show me," Duncan said as he came to stand next to her.

When he saw where it was, he said, "Right let's go pay them a visit."

Raine returned to the new base to be met by Robbins who asked, "Where did you go to? You left without any back-up."

"I had something to take care of," he replied.

"Keeping secrets are we now then?" Robbins noticed.

"No, I didn't tell you because you didn't need to know," Raine told him looking him straight in the eye almost as if he was daring him to challenge him over it. He was in charge still and he was just letting him know.

"Okay, I get it, just be careful if you need to make any more trips, I don't need to know about, just make sure the location is secure and your exfil is clear. We're too far into this now to make simple mistakes like that," Robbins said.

"Point taken and on that same note, I am instituting a slight change of plans. I want all the targets hit at the same time. The original plan was to hit them one after the other, seeing as how they think we're dead, if we continued with that plan, they'd soon figure out who was responsible and then try to stop us again. It won't work but it could delay us. So, if we hit them all simultaneously, they won't be able to stop it from happening."

"When do you want to start?" Robbins asked.

"Right away, there's no time like the present," Raine said with a sly grin.

"I'll get right on it, the samples will be ready in the hour," Robbins said about to leave for the lab.

"No need, it's all ready to go, I checked earlier. The rockets are loaded and are just waiting for the target vectors to be loaded into the computer and we're good to go."

Raine could see by Robbins furrowed brow he was concerned by all of this. He'd already expressed his concerns over continuing. He was afraid the Coalition would never stop looking for them, no matter where they went after what they were about to do, and he was right. Those were valid concerns. If being in the military had taught him anything it was that they did not ever negotiate with threats from any source. Criminals and terrorists alike were hunted down and destroyed with a focus that bordered on obsessive.

What Robbins was unaware of though was that he had taken steps to nullify that protocol. In one fell swoop he would kill two birds with one stone and ensure his freedom at the same time. He'd purposely neglected to inform his second in command after his recent outburst because if he knew what this part of his plan was, he would never go along with it.

Before there was time for any further conversation he said, "Time to go and make some history my friend. Let's go change the world forever," he said as he got up and left.

Chapter 38

"You weren't serious about paying these guys an actual visit, were you?" Sanchez asked as they left the city in the Nimbus.

Duncan glanced her way then returned his gaze to the road ahead, saying nothing.

"I mean, there will be somewhere upwards of a hundred of his followers there, all armed and not too friendly towards outsiders. If you hadn't noticed, that's the two of us," she continued.

Finally, he said, "Calm down, we're going to be alright, trust me."

"Oh well now you got me worried because when anyone says 'trust me' you know exactly the opposite of they say is going to happen, happens," she replied a little more animatedly than before.

Stopping the car he turned to her, "If you want to go home, get out now otherwise shut the fuck up and let's get the job done," he said looking her directly in the eye, his face a mask of cold hard determination.

"You're crazy, did anyone ever tell you that, crazy that's what you are?" she said, her eyes wider than normal. As if she was seeing him for the first time.

Duncan hit a switch on the arm rest and the passenger side door released and swung open.

"Oh, hell no, you are not leaving me at no roadside like some roadkill," she said grabbing the door and slamming it shut once more. "Go on, drive you crazy fool, someone's got to watch your back or you're more than likely to wander into something you can't get out of and where does that leave the mission 'eh?" she snapped at him, then turned to stare straight ahead as she waited for him to move the car along.

Duncan began driving once more and he heard her mutter something under her breath that sounded like, "You crazy mutherfucka."

He couldn't help but smile because he knew her fears were unfounded, he had no intention of actually visiting the militia compound but he wasn't about to tell her that, not yet at least. She had irritated him throughout the mission with her incessant questions and constantly talking so he thought he would give her a taste of what it was like.

They continued in silence until they reached the spot he had chosen and he stopped the car once more.

Looking around Sanchez asked, "Why are we stopping here?"

Duncan operated something on the dash and a hidden compartment in the rear of the car opened up and a small fleet of drones took off. To the naked eye they appeared to be a swarm of flies but in fact they were tiny robots, remotely controlled by the AI with cameras fitted to them which were used for surveillance when it was impossible, or too dangerous to get close to a target without being seen.

As the screen on the dash lit up showing various images from the cameras Sanchez said, "You devious sonofabitch, you played me."

"If you remember, I never actually said we were going to visit personally," he argued knowing full well that his argument held as much water as a leaky bucket.

"Nicely played Agent Pryde, you had me going for a second there. Tell me, what would you have done had I got out of the car when you pulled over?"

"Why, driven off, of course. The mission comes first, if you'd have gotten out it would have proven to me you are not cut out for field work such as this. You never take anything on face value, you never trust anyone and the mission always comes first," he replied with a straight face.

"So, it was a test and not a wind up then?"

Breaking into a hint of a smile Duncan said, "Just a little bit of a prank, I have to admit. Well, you are so annoying and such a distraction I thought it time I paid you back a little."

"Again, with the distraction," she said and he suspected she would continue with this so he pointed at the screen, "Look, they're nearing the militia compound," he said to divert her attention.

Unfortunately, it didn't work, she said, "Agent Pryde, this conversation is not over."

"Can we concentrate for just a minute here?" Duncan said wanting to get back on track. He looked at the screen to see the video feed from the flies. They showed the compound from above.

It was roughly square shaped with a large fence erected around it. On each corner was a guard tower which stood thirty feet above the fence giving them a three-hundred-and-sixty-degree view of the surrounding area. Inside the compound were a number of habitats used as living quarters and another, larger one probably used as an armoury. In the centre was one habitat which appeared to be either Kaufman's or it was used as a central meeting/conference place, from this angle it was hard to make out which.

They could see the three choppers they had arrived in parked at the rear of the compound along with several ground vehicles including a large armoured troop carrier.

A quick estimate of how many figures could be seen put it at close to one hundred men and women, again it was difficult to get an accurate number due to them moving around, in and out of the habitats.

Sanchez looked at Duncan and said, "Okay Agent Pryde, what's our next move?"

Returning her look, and with a straight face, announced, "I have a plan, but you're not going to like it."

Rolling her eyes she sighed, "How did I know you were going to say that."

Chapter 39

I n the control room Raine watched as preparations for the final phase of his plan were put into action.

Looking through the window from the observation level they could see the rockets lined up pointing up to the ceiling all ready to be fired. One rocket for each of the immigration sites, twelve in all.

"What happened to the shuttles that were going to disperse the virus into the air over the campsites then? Robbins asked when he saw the delivery system.

"Change of plan. Using rockets will be more efficient and faster," Raine admitted.

"You're really going to do this aren't you?" Robbins said at his side when he saw the rockets.

Turning to look at his friend he said, "Of course, did you ever doubt it?"

"I suppose I always thought you would do something, but not this slaughter."

"You shared the same view as I did about how our government betrayed us, giving over some of our land to those immigrants. You hate them as much as I do, so what has changed?"

"There are women and children in those camps. All they want is a second chance, they don't deserve to die like this," Robbins argued.

"They destroyed their own homeworld, what's to say they won't do something like that here. Not only did they destroy their world but made the entire star system unstable. I'm not going to allow that kind of thing happen here. They have to learn there are consequences to their actions."

"I know there are, but do they have to die for it?"

"What would you have me do? How severe should the punishment be?" Raine asked.

"I agree they should face some punishment but to slaughter them all is not our job. We have no right to take their lives like that."

"Who is, our government? Let's be serious here, the government is the one body of authority who agreed to their being placed here and the Coalition Council ordered it. What punishment have they given them, none, not even a slap on the wrist. They have gotten away with it so what have they learned? I'll tell you; they now know they can destroy a world and other people will rescue them and give them another home. Let me ask you, is that right?"

Robbins had no answer for that he just dropped his gaze to the floor unable to look Raine in the eye any longer. He understood what Raine's argument was but he couldn't come up with an alternative to it. He knew it was wrong to kill them all but on the other hand he couldn't allow it to go unpunished. It was a complex argument that he had no solution for. Finally, he said, "You're right Marcus, this should not go unpunished but at least warn the government of your intensions first, at least give them a chance to repair the damage they have done. See if they can come up with a solution that will give us what we want without the need for bloodshed."

"What good would that do? They made their decision without consulting the population, as if we had no say in the matter. They never considered what we thought about it all, didn't care about the impact the sudden increase in population would have on our ecology. It was simply made and we were expected to suck it up and carry on. Let me ask you another question, if our homeworld reaches the point where it cannot sustain the population do you think the government and the elite members of our society will suffer? I'll tell you the answer to that, it's quite simple. The answer is no, they will just move to another world where their money and status will ensure they are looked after. They don't give a fuck about us; we have to look after ourselves because they sure won't."

Robbins actually saw the sense in what his friend said and nodded his agreement.

"Besides if we warn them, they'll know for sure we are alive and what we plan on doing, I'm not giving them that advantage."

"Okay, point taken," Robbins said, "as long as you've thought it through then and this is not some spur of the moment thing and you're acting out of anger."

"My friend, if there is one thing about this, I can assure you it is that I have thought it through. In fact, I've thought of nothing else since the decision was made. I have looked at it from every conceivable angle until I could not see any other way to deal with it. I don't take this decision lightly; I will bear the horror of what is about to happen to my grave but it must be done to ensure the safety of our world."

"I may not have your clarity of purpose Marcus, but I will stand by your side through to the bitter end, you have my word."

Turning his attention back to the launch pad Raine gave the order to fire.

There was no turning back now.

Chapter 40

"Are you serious?" Sanchez asked.

"If you can think of another way then I'm all ears, if not then we're with this plan," he told her with a straight face.

See stared at him then had to glance away as she obviously had no other ideas. Frustrated by that fact made it worse as well. Having to concede that to him felt like a much bigger deal than it should and she wondered if he had gotten under her skin as much as he had said she had under his.

That couldn't be true, could it? I mean he's a total psycho, okay he was cute but he was as unfeeling as a chunk of granite. This and more went through her mind which also surprised her, instead of trying to come up with an alternative all she could think about how much she liked those eyes of his.

"Okay, so just because I can't think of another plan doesn't mean we should just go ahead with a suicidal one," she admitted finally.

"Well, I'm not choosing to sit around and waiting. We need to find out where Kaufman and his men fit into this. If we can learn from them where Raine is then I'll certainly take the chance."

"Shit, fuck!" she swore adding, "okay let's get it done. Who wants to live forever anyway?"

"Veronica, I don't intend on dying today, or any day. I don't have a death wish, no matter what you think," Duncan said looking in the eye to let her know he meant what he said.

"I really hope you're right about that Duncan, I honestly do because I've grown attached to my life and I wouldn't like it to end any time soon," she told him holding his gaze.

"Okay, let's go," he said.

"Sir, I just picked up twelve signals on the sensors, travelling at speed toward several areas in or near the cities across the planet," ops said. The Situation Room in the Council head-quarters had been on full alert since the incident at the facility when the Omega Five virus had been stolen. The Council Leader, Governor Goldstein was eager to appear as if they had the situation under complete control.

Goldstein was a career politician and knew the unrest that was building on his world. Allowing the immigrants to be placed on Altair was not a decision he took lightly. It was either allow it or face the consequences. President Harada had made it perfectly clear that there would be repercussions, nothing as simple as being blacklisted but their position on the trade register would certainly suffer. They would get supplies but they would be so far down the list that they might as well be on their own.

"What are they and where are they heading, I want specifics man," Goldstein said. He was standing at the head of the table unable to sit any longer. He had been the head of the government for the past three years and this was the largest crisis he'd had to deal with. At sixty-three years old his advancing years had begun to show in the wrinkles around his eyes and across his tall forehead. Being the head of the government meant he had little time to exercise as regularly as he'd liked and his thickening waistline was evidence of that.

At the far end of the room was a bank of monitors with an impressive screen mounted on the wall taking centre stage. A row of desks was arranged in front of it where workers sat keeping an eye on things happening around the planet.

"They appear to be rockets sir all heading for what looks like the immigration campsites."

Turning to the leader of the Altair military, General Grey, he said, "What can this mean?"

General Grey was as perplexed as the governor. With a shrug of his shoulders he said, "I have no clue sir."

"Get me surveillance over those campsites, I want to see what the hell is going on out there," Goldstein ordered as he began pacing the width of the room. He had a terrible feeling this had something to do with the theft of that virus he'd been informed of, and the suspicion of the Ministry that Marcus Raine had some involvement in it. But that couldn't be right, could it, after all, Raine was reported killed, wasn't he?

All these thoughts danced around in the politician's head as he wondered how this would affect his term of office. If this did have something to do with Raine and that damned virus then he would be remembered for all time as the man who did nothing to prevent a crisis of unimaginable consequences.

Turning back to the general he said, "Grey, I want troops sent to each campsite. I want those immigrants protected. If anything happens to them then the shit really will hit the fan around here. Get it done General and get it done now."

Unsure of what he could really do to help at this late stage against simultaneous rocket attacks he instead said, "Copy that sir, I'll get right on it."

He left the room already contacting his men to deploy to the campsites.

Inside the room Goldstein asked, "How soon before those rockets reach their targets?"

"Less than ten minutes sir," came the answer and he realised he had reacted too late. The troops would never reach them in time to erect any kind of defence from the incoming rockets.

Sitting back down at the head of the table he held his head in his hands as he waited for the inevitable hoping he was wrong though.

Chapter 41

Duncan had taken the Nimbus closer to the compound under a camouflage shield. The vehicle blended in with the surroundings and would pass any casual scrutiny from observers.

Inside the vehicle Duncan and Sanchez both wore their camouflage battle suits made from the fluid body armour.

They were ready to go.

"Don't worry, as long as we're quick and remain calm then the chances are good, we won't be seen," Duncan told her after seeing the fear opening her eyes. She was biting her lip as the tension was getting to her. Credit to her though, as afraid as she was, she was still going through with his plan, she would face the same dangers as he would and that was a mark of true courage. For the first time since they had begun working together, he realised what a badass she really was.

"I would prefer it if the chances were great, good just doesn't instil that much confidence in me," she replied. Taking a final deep breath, she said, "let's do this before I change my mind."

Exiting the car through the rear door they would not disturb the camouflage shield and remain undetected. Keeping low they proceeded toward the compound.

It didn't matter which side they breached as each side was covered by the guard tower on the corner of the compound. Up in the tower was a guard armed with a Sabre G300 AAR probably configured for the assault rifle mode. They had an uninterrupted view of the area surrounding the compound which at times made them slightly too relaxed. No one in their right mind would attempt to approach them without being seen and then challenged so they were confident they were quite safe.

Duncan used a small laser cutter and cut through the bottom of the fence hoping that it wasn't linked to some alarm and that they relied solely on the watch towers to raise any alarm.

He had a hole cut through in seconds large enough for the two of them to pass through, one at a time.

Inside the fence they moved toward one of the habitats.

As they reached it there was a sudden increase in activity around the compound. They saw weapons being passed around and more people went toward the fence to take up positions.

Something had happened. At first Duncan thought they had been alerted of the breach in the fence but as no one seemed to go in that direction he realised it was something else entirely.

"What's going on?" Sanchez whispered through the comm link.

"I have no idea but whatever it is, it doesn't look good," he replied.

As he looked around, he saw that there was a concentration of forces against the fence which meant the habitats would be left unguarded or empty.

"Whatever is going on it may just work to our advantage," he said and as he walked off around the habitat they had been using as cover he added, "Are you coming or what?"

The two of them kept to the outside of the compound moving slowly in and out of the habitats until they came to the one Duncan had been looking for.

Opening the door Duncan noticed it was empty inside. Stepping through the door he went over to the centre console that had a computer terminal integrated inside. Taking out his PIN he attached it to the computer wirelessly then began searching through all the files. He was searching for any connection to Raine. The connection also gave a record of all the communications in and out of the compound.

He noticed one that had been routed through a secure link to Kaufman personally. When he ran the incoming call through his database, he found it to be from somewhere in the Wasteland.

Another signal alerted him to what might be behind the recent increase in activity.

Sanchez watched over the door while he worked at the computer, when he walked over to her, she said, "That was quick."

"We have to go," he replied.

"Why, what's happened?"

Without looking at her, he said, "It's begun."

Chapter 42

The nearest campsite to the launch site was alerted by the authorities.

The campsite co-ordinator, Gordon Wexler was present at the time as it was his job to ensure everything ran smoothly for the people being placed at each campsite until permanent housing could be procured for them.

As soon as the call came through, he went outside to see if he could see anything and as soon as he looked up and saw the rocket, his heart sank.

The campsite, as all the others, was a simple hastily erected number of tents set up as a temporary home to all those fleeing the dead planet that was their previous home. None of these campsites had any defences so when Wexler saw the rocket, he knew exactly what was going to happen and he ran. Not thinking nor caring about anyone else, his only thought then was of escape and his own survival.

The other people in the camp saw this reaction and watched, dumbstruck as he ran for the edge of the campsite. He had travelled here in a small shittle that was supposed to pick him up at a prearranged time later that day so his only recourse was to escape on foot.

Seeing him running, they too looked up to see what had startled him. When they saw the rocket, it was too late for them to do anything but scream.

The rocket detonated in the air above the campsite and a fine mist dispersed over the entire area spread farther by the shockwave caused by the detonation.

At first the residents cheered as the relief from escaping what they thought was a certain death washed over them just as the fine mist did. When they realised this wasn't what it seemed at first, their reactions turned to one of bewilderment at first, and then horror.

Within the first few minutes, people started showing symptoms. It was different for everyone but the results were the same, a slow and agonizing death.

Wexler felt the mist touch him and he began to panic, his pace slowed as he tried to brush off the damp mist from his bare flesh. Panic made him react the way he had. He had expected something, anything but this. When he realised his removal of the damp particles from him had no effect, he questioned what this was. Who would send a rocket at them with this inside if it had no effect? It didn't make any sense, none of it did. Finally, he stopped running and turned to look at the campsite, what he saw chilled him to the bone. He watched as people started falling over, some had blood pouring from their mouths, noses and other orifices. Others had skin peeling from their faces where the mist had landed on them. It was horrific to watch and he felt his stomach churn. He checked his own body once more just to be sure, his own eyes could be deceiving him, but saw no reaction.

What did that mean?

He remained on the edge unable to walk, to move at all as his eyes were transfixed on the horror happening before him.

Whatever it was it has spared him. He had no idea why or how but he was just glad that it had. He fell to the ground and wept, his head in his hands as death continued to spread inside the camp.

The other camps suffered the same fate as the first one. The death toll rose as more and more of the rockets dispersed their deadly cargo of the genetically altered Omega Five virus.

Back at Kaufman's compound Duncan and Sanchez knew something had happened, but they had no idea of the enormity of it.

"We need to get back to the car and get out of here," Duncan said as they exited the habitat.

"Are we going out the way we came in?" Sanchez asked.

"We'll have to, there is no other way to go."

"I was afraid you'd say that."

"Keep calm and we'll be fine."

"That's easy for you to say, you who can control his emotions. The rest of us don't have that luxury."

"Good job I'm here to hold your hand then, isn't it?" Duncan told her.

"Agent Pryde, this is not the right time or place to be flirting with me," she said keeping her face as straight as possible. Duncan knew then she would be good. If she could tell jokes in the middle of a dangerous situation, he knew she had herself under control.

They moved back toward the fence and the entry point careful not to alert all the men and women running around getting ready for whatever they thought was coming.

"What's that?" a voice shouted off to the side somewhere deep in the camp.

Duncan froze for an instant. He slowly moved his head to look at who had spoken, careful not to move too quickly so that the camouflage suit wouldn't be detected. He saw someone pointing right at the two of them.

He knew in that instant their cover had been blown.

"Run!" he shouted and he took off for the fence.

Bullets traced his path as the shooters tried to target him. His sudden run had thrown off their aim slightly but it was simply a matter of time before they zeroed in on their target. He wouldn't be able to evade their shots forever.

Sanchez ran at his side her gun drawn as she returned fire. This brought more attention from the shooters onto her. Duncan turned and fired several shots at the first of the gunners, dropping the first three and forcing the others to take cover.

They still had to get through the fence and beyond. This wasn't going to be easy.

He ran for the fence as the ground behind him was chewed up by bullets.

Sanchez was at his side as a group of soldiers at the fence turned to face them. At least ten guns were aimed directly at the two of them. With nowhere to turn, they stopped.

"Who do we have here?" a deep bass voice asked from behind them.

A large red headed man walked up to the two of them.

"Nice suits," he said looking them up and down. Being this close to them he could actually see them and he tore off the head covering of the nearest one revealing Sanchez's face.

"Well, I didn't see that coming," he admitted.

Turning to the other figure he snatched that covering off too.

"That, I expected," he said. "Now what are you two idiots doing here, clearly not anything good I assume?"

Duncan glanced at his partner and the large man said, "Before we go any further, let's have those guns, shall we? Tell Kaufman we have them."

"Copy that," said the man Tate had spoken to.

Duncan reacted first.

He brought up his pistol and fired at the man closest to Tate. The large calibre bullet hit him in the face destroying it instantly snapping his head back.

Sanchez fired next dropping two more of the ten facing them. Tate charged at Duncan grabbing him around the waist and slamming him into the fence. His men parted to allow the charge to go through them.

Duncan felt pain explode across his back as he collided with the fence. The huge bear of a man was still holding him and he tried to bring his gun up to fire but his arm was blocked.

He butted Tate on the nose smashing it. Blood spread out as his head was rocked back and he instinctively released his grip on Duncan. Pushing the giant away from him Duncan delivered a snap kick to the knee collapsing the leg. Following up with a roundhouse kick to the side of the head Duncan felt his leg grabbed. Before he knew what was happening the big man was standing up holding his leg before swinging him bodily away from the fence a few feet.

Duncan landed heavily on the ground and got back up immediately. He had total control of his emotions now that the battle had started in earnest. He looked at the man facing him, his face devoid of expression despite the blood running down into his mouth from the damaged nose. He knew the man was bigger and stronger than him and probably had training in the Open Combat system the same as himself. Most military and Special Forces groups trained in this system which basically was a mix of whatever worked, martial arts, boxing, grappling, dirty tricks, if it got the job done, then it was used, but he didn't have his singular focus. He would be willing to kill to end this but he was angry which gave Duncan the advantage. When anger entered into any fight it froze the mind into acting on pure rage. That could be Duncan's only advantage here, a slight one admittedly but an advantage none the less because he was thinking logically, planning out his strategy.

He saw the shock in his eyes at him getting back up so fast. He eyed him up seeing him go into a fighting stance, balanced evenly on both feet so he did the same.

Sanchez was having her own problems with the others. They came at her forcing her to shoot as many as she could. She dropped three more before the rest grabbed her. She fought like a hellcat punching and kicking her way out of the group.

She had four men to contend with so she used her agility to her best advantage, trying to keep out of range and pick her shots. She didn't see what was happening with her partner, she was concentrating hard on staying alive. One thing she did know was if they didn't get out of here fast, others would soon join the fight and then escape would be impossible.

Tate attacked Duncan, fuelled by his anger. Duncan saw the move and reacted fast. The punch went over his right shoulder as he dipped it bringing his right arm up in an uppercut which connected with Kaufman's chin rocking his head up and back. Following up with a left cross he struck him on the side of his face snapping his head sideways.

Tate recovered fast and shoulder charged Duncan away from him then tackled him around the waist slamming him into the ground. He was on top of him then raising a fist to hit him. The first punch glanced off the side of his face cutting his cheek. He couldn't move his head fast enough to evade being hit.

Pain exploded across his face and he knew he couldn't take a punch full on like that without it stunning him. He saw another punch coming and tried to move again. The blow hit him on the side again, this time near his temple and his vision was suddenly filled with exploding stars.

He knew this was the first step to him blacking out and he had to do something. He felt his strength ebbing and he pulled all his reserves together for one final push.

He got a hand free and jabbed the big man in the throat with a straight fingers jab. No matter how big or strong a person was, a jab to the throat will stop anyone. Tate may have been built like a brick shithouse with muscles in places where most people don't have places but, just like normal people his throat was vulnerable. He reeled from the blow like anyone else would. His hands immediately went to his throat as he found his airlines constricted.

Duncan was then able to move him off him and scramble to his feet. Dragging air into his lungs Duncan got his breathing back under control and faced his giant attacker once mor.

The fury in Tate's eyes was that of a wild animal. Duncan hit him in the face with a left jab then a straight right with as much force as he could muster. Both punches hit the same eye and he saw the swelling begin almost immediately.

As Tate moved forward, Duncan hit him between the legs with a front snap kick doubling him over in agony.

Taking his knife out from the sheath strapped to his right thigh he slashed the blade across Tate's throat. A jet of blood spurted out from the severed carotid. His hands went up to the wound hoping to stem the flow. Duncan thrust the blade into his ribs near the kidneys and then slashed one thigh then the other. Tate was now bleeding out fast and he dropped to his knees before falling face first on the ground.

Sanchez was fighting a group of men on her own and Duncan threw his blade into the back of the neck of one of them.

He raced over to lend a hand yanking his blade free from the body then slashed sideways at the one on his right catching him across the neck.

Sanchez punched another in the face, gave the other a side-kick in the ribs knocking him flat.

Grabbing her hand Duncan pulled her toward the fence and pushed her through the hole before anyone else could join the fracas.

As they ran Duncan said, "Car get the engine started, we're coming in hot."

Chapter 43

By the time they had sprinted to where the car was a group had already begun the chase firing as they ran.

Bullets kicked up sand as they missed the target but it didn't deter the two agents from running. In fact, it spurred on their efforts.

The car was already running when they arrived, they quickly climbed in slamming the doors allowing the AI to drive them away until they had got settled in their seats.

The tyres kicked up twin plumes of sand high into the air as it sped away. Bullets peppered the rear of the car to no avail; the bodywork had been reinforced to withstand small arms fire.

A chopper was in the air coming after them also.

"Car, target that aircraft," Duncan said as he saw it on the screen that showed what was behind them.

"Target locked Commander."

Heavy calibre shells struck the ground on either side of the car from the twin rotary cannons mounted either side of the chopper.

The chopper then fired a salvo of rockets at the car. The AI steered the car out of the way just in time. The rockets hit the ground in front of them and exploded sending up a shower of fiery shrapnel and sand cascading down in an orange torrent.

The car fired a rocket at the chopper blowing it out of the sky, when the wreckage hit the ground, it caused a barricade between the car and anyone following.

Duncan took the wheel and headed out of the Wastelands at the best possible speed.

"That was damn close," Sanchez admitted once they were clear and the members of the militia had given up their chase.

Duncan wiped blood away from his face with the back of his hand then concentrated on his driving.

"Commander I have been monitoring comm chatter and there have been reports of an attack on all twelve immigrant campsites.," the AI said.

Duncan and Sanchez shared a glance.

"It's happened," she said voicing the dread they were both feeling.

"We need to find Raine, and fast," Duncan said.

At that particular moment Raine and Robbins along with a select number of his men had left the base and were heading into the city.

"It's all over the news feeds, all of the campsites were hit and the refugees are all dead. You did it Marcus, you actually did it," Robbins said.

"And now to finish this off," Raine said.

"What do you mean, where are we going?" Robbins asked.

"To deliver my message in person," Raine said.

Robbins glanced over his shoulder at the rows of men sitting behind them. They were in a shuttle that had taken off from inside the base and was now high over the Wastelands.

"Do they know where we are going, what have you told them?" Robbins asked.

"Now Mykel, don't go soft on me. This is the part that cements our place in history and ensures that we make our way forward and protect our homeworld. What we do toady will change the course of our history forever," Raine told him quietly.

"I just hope you know what you're doing," Robbins said as quietly as before.

"We'll soon find out, we're coming in over the city," Raine said.

The Council chambers were in shock over the attacks on the immigration campsites.

No one could believe such a thing could happen on their world. Things like this happened on other worlds, on frontier worlds where the rule of law has yet to be made stable. Not here, not on their world.

All eyes remained staring at the monitor screen showing footage of the devastation in the campsites. All the deaths, bodies lying on the ground in various stages and states of death was shocking to see. Yet they couldn't tear their eyes from the spectacle.

"Who could do such a thing?" the Governor asked with tears filling his eyes blurring his vision.

"We have to find out who was responsible for this atrocity," General Grey said his face set in determination.

"This must not go unpunished General, we cannot allow this to pass without at least doing something," Goldstein said.

"I'll do what I can sir," Grey said then left the Situation Room.

With all the commotion and shock from seeing twelve campsites attacked no one noticed a shuttle entering the Council Chambers restricted airspace until the alarm sounded.

"What is that?" Goldstein asked tearing his eyes from the large monitor for the first time.

"We have a shuttle inbound sir," replied the officer manning the sensors.

"Are our defences alerted?" he asked.

"Sir, whoever they are, they've just opened fire on us."

Chapter 44

"Commander, I am getting readings of an incident at the government council building. It seems they are under attack sir," the AI in the Nimbus reported.

"Raine, it has to be," Duncan said. "We need to get there and fast," he added.

The AI said, "In that case Commander I would suggest you hold on tight."

The car continued on but inside the two passengers could hear something happening to it.

"What the fuck is that?" Sanchez said looking around to see if she could spot where the noise was coming from.

Under the car, thrusters fired lifting it off the ground into a low hover until the wheels rotated inwards so the sides were facing downwards. The wheel hub opened up and powerful engines fired lifting the car off the ground into the air. As soon as the nose was pointing upwards the rear main engine kicked in and the car became a flying aircraft.

"Holy sit, you never told me this thing could do that," Sanchez scolded him.

"Sorry, it never came up," Duncan replied as he steered the car up into the air high enough to see the city in the distance.

Behind them the compound was still a hive of activity. Duncan said, "Car, target the armoury, let's see if we can't put those guys out of business."

"Copy that Commander," the AI responded and as the car continued to rise rockets fired from the rear pods aimed at the compound below.

The rockets streaked toward their target and hit the large tent that housed all the munitions for the militia group. The effect was instantaneous. A huge explosion mushroomed outward destroying the tent in a massive fireball which sent debris flying in all directions. This explosion was just the beginning though. The munitions being stored there, explosives, ammunition and everything else a militia would need, was detonated in a firework display that could be seen for miles around.

Anyone caught in the blast would be incinerated instantly and those farther away would be torn apart by the shockwave that spread out faster than they could evade.

No one would be left alive down there and if by some chance they did survive, they would be in no fit state to mount a chase.

"That was emphatic," Sanchez said once the display had ended.

"I think they got the point," agreed Duncan.

Their speed increased close to the speed of sound as they headed for the council buildings.

"Let's hope we're in time to help," Duncan said as he faced the struggle ahead.

There was nothing to add to that so Sanchez simply kept quiet and held on.

Inside the council chambers the atmosphere had darkened as reports started to filter through about the immigration campsites being attacked.

Goldstein was devastated as the death toll mounted. The details about only the immigrants being targeted.

"What are we doing about these attacks?" he said.

General Grey said, "I've dispatched troops to each campsite sir along with Hazmat teams and first responders."

"That's all well and good General but what are we doing about who fired those weapons?"

"We are trying to back track where they were fired from but so far it's proving to be problematic."

"In what way General?"

"It seems as if they were fired from somewhere inside the Wastelands, that's as far as our signals traced them to sir."

"The Wastelands? That's a massive area to search. Is there any way to narrow the target area down?"

"We're working on it sir," Grey said a little too sheepishly for the Governor.

"Work on it faster General, this is a disaster and we have to do everything we can to minimise the outcome. We may not be able to do anything about those poor souls who died but we sure can make sure the bastards responsible are brought to justice," he said.

"Copy that sir," Grey said and he was about to say something else when another voice broke into the conversation.

"Sir we have an incoming shuttle."

Grey said, "Clarify, what kind of shuttle and how did it get through our sensor perimeter?"

"As far as I can tell sir they gave an active access code. It landed on the landing pad near here sir."

"Are they hostile?" Goldstein asked looking from the general to the technician.

"There's no way of knowing sir."

Goldstein turned to the general and said, "Well don't you think you should go and find out then?"

"Copy that," he said and went to leave the room.

"I want eyes on that shuttle. We need to know who they are and what their intentions are," Goldstein said turning back to the technician.

"I have that sir," he replied indicating the main monitor. It displayed the landing pad and the shuttle parked there. It was of a military configuration capable of carrying troops.

As they watched a group of men and women came out, all armed with assault rifles. One of them led the party and looked straight up at the camera overlooking the landing pad and smiled then waved for those watching.

"That's Marcus Raine," Goldstein said open mouthed, "The bastard's not dead after all." He added.

Chapter 45

Raine led his team toward the Council Building.

He and Robbins led the way with the rest of them following, four of them carrying a large crate between them.

As they continued toward the building six of his men moved around Raine and Robbins, three on either side to for an honour guard to protect their flanks. The three stone steps up to the front entrance to the building were wide with supporting columns of marble holding up the overhanging roof.

Three guards appeared with rifles to challenge the newcomers but before they could say more than the obligatory 'freeze' a salvo of bullets from the men flanking the main group tore them apart. The three guards fell to the floor dead, leaving the way clear for Raine to enter.

Raine wore a cruel grin as he walked through the door to the building. The lobby was spacious with a large wide staircase that wound up to the upper floors in a circular fashion. The reception desk was situated in the middle with a marble counter which was circular and the receptionist sat in the middle, surveying everyone who came and went.

At the moment it was empty, having been vacated when the alert went out.

"You know what to do?" Raine said as he stood in the lobby looking around. He noticed several doors leading off the lobby and pointed to his men to cover them. He knew where he was going and it wasn't on this floor.

There was another staircase that led down to the basement levels, one of which was where the Situation Room and the Bunker was situated.

"Go," he said and his men started down the staircase. Raine followed on after the four carrying the case.

They went down to the basement and as they entered the floor a corridor opened out from the stairway door. At the end of this was a large double door guarded by two security guards. As soon as they saw them the men with Raine opened fire. The gunfire knocked the two bodies back onto the double doors and they fell to the floor.

"Okay guys, let's get in there," Raine said. The doors were opened and his men burst in with guns up ready to fire.

Guards inside turned to face the intrusion and were cut down by gunfire from the doorway.

"Governor Goldstein, it's so nice to see you," Raine said smiling broadly.

Indicating the floor at the head of the table he added, "Place it down, right there will do."

"What do you want Raine?" Goldstein asked standing back at the front of the room away from all the men brandishing the guns.

"I've come to deliver this, it's a little present which I'm sure you'll appreciate," Raine replied.

All eyes in the room turned to look at the crate that had been brought in with them.

Dreading the answer, Goldstein asked, "What's that?"

Raine looked at him and his smile disappeared as he said, "I like to think of it as justice."

"As soon as we touch down, we move, got that?" Duncan said as the car came in to land on the landing pad next to the shuttle.

"Copy that," Sanchez replied and he could tell by the firm set of her jaw and the cold stare in her eyes, she was ready for this.

They could see the front of the building where three men were standing guard on the steps by the marble columns. As soon as they saw them the guards stepped behind the columns.

The cover leading up to the steps was minimal, in fact non-existent. It was nothing more than open ground between the landing pad and the entrance to the building.

Even though they were in the heart of the city there was a large courtyard surrounding it which included the landing pad and car park.

Duncan and Sanchez separated immediately going to opposite directions. Bullets chased them across the ground threatening to carve them up.

Duncan returned fire as he ran, his bullets sent sparks flying from where they struck the columns. Sanchez did the same with more or less the same result.

They each reached the corner of the building and disappeared around it. Bullets pinged off the corner sending concrete chips flying into the air.

Standing at the corner Duncan could see the targets beside the columns. As he peered around the corner, he fired off a quick shot. The bullet struck the column forcing the guard to move back behind for safety.

He knew Sanchez was doing the same from her side. He had to be careful not to get hit in a crossfire from his partner.

Needing to get inside as fast as possible he took a chance.

"Wait for my signal," he said to Sanchez through the commlink.

"Copy that," she replied as she peered around the corner.

Duncan took out a grenade, primed it then tossed it at the entrance. The small object bounced onto the steps then rolled toward the entrance before exploding. The blast cracked the columns and killed the three guards, shredding their bodies.

Tentatively, Duncan made his way toward the entrance, his gun aimed at the three bodies. A glance up told him Sanchez was doing the same. One look at the remains was enough to ensure no life remained there.

Blood and body parts were strewn across the entrance and Duncan stepped over them with little regard for what it was as he went to the front doors. Sanchez followed on behind him as they entered the building.

Chapter 46

"What's that supposed to mean, justice?" Goldstein asked incensed by the intrusion.

Raine walked over to the crate and lifted the lid. Inside was a canister that had a device attached. at one end with a timer attached. Beneath the cannister was an explosive device and it was obvious to anyone looking on what this was meant to do.

"I think you know exactly what it means Governor, so let's not play coy here," Raine said.

Robbins leaned in to say something, "We just lost contact with the guards at the front."

Raine looked at him then around the room. All the people who should be here were down at the front with just Goldstein and General Grey close to him. He looked at Robbins and said, "You stay here Mykel and keep this place secure. I'll take some of the men and go check this out. I'll be back soon."

Before Robbins could comment Raine had signalled to three of the men and was leaving Robbins with the rest of the team.

"You heard the man, no one gets in or out of here until he returns," Robbins said making sure his men knew what to do.

All attention was on everyone inside the room when Robbins heard the door close behind after Raine had left. As it closed, he heard the lock snap closed sealing them inside with the rest of them.

Disregarding it as simply nothing more than a precaution to ensure no one got past them he continued to keep his attention on what was happening inside the room.

———

Raine closed and sealed the door behind them locking it securely.

"That should do it. Sorry Mykel, you should never have informed me of your doubts about this, that sealed your fate," he said as he walked away from the locked door. He had no intention of returning there and he reached for his PIN and activated the remote timer that would set off the bomb.

"Let's go, we need to get as far away from here as we can, just in case," he said to the team.

———

Inside the room, Robbins caught a glimpse of something in the corner of his eye. Something flashing red coming from the crate.

He glanced down and saw the timer had been activated and was counting down.

They had ten minutes and counting before this thing went off.

Trying not to alert the rest of the men he backed up to the door and tried to open it. To his dismay, but not totally unexpected he found it locked. Through his com link he called Raine.

"Marcus, what're you doing?" he said as quietly as he could. He'd motioned for the team to herd the occupants together at the front of the room so he wouldn't be heard. The last thing he wanted was a mass panic on his hands. All control over the room was lost if they found out they were trapped inside a sealed room with a bomb.

"I don't know what you mean Mykel," Raine replied.

"The timer has been activated and the doors are locked. Tell me you didn't do this Marcus," he said but deep down in his heart he knew the truth.

"I'm sorry Mykel, I can't do that," Raine said confirming Robbins' suspicions.

"You sonofabitch, why, why have you done this?" Robbins asked

"Don't play coy with me Mykel, you know very well why. What, did you think I'd let your comments earlier go unchallenged?"

"Is that it, because I questioned the sanity of killing all those people, you do this?"

"You were with me until this shit got real which wasn't good enough Mykel. You were going to turn against me so I made sure you couldn't."

"What do you mean I was going to turn against you, I went along with the launches against the immigration campsites, didn't I? Wasn't that enough proof for you that I was on your side?"

"Yes, you did go along but I couldn't take the chance that at some point you'd have a change of heart. This is too important for that Mykel. Instead, you can take solace at the knowledge that you've helped shape the future of our homeworld. You won't be around to see it all but you will be remembered fondly, I promise you that. Goodbye Mykel," Raines said and closed the call.

The others in the room suspected something was wrong and one of them asked, "Is everything alright Boss?"

Robbins lowered his rifle and said, "We're all gonna die."

Chapter 47

"Where are they?" Sanchez asked as they entered the lobby of the building.

There were bodies lying around, evidence of Raines intrusion but no signs of anyone else.

"The Situation Room will be in a safe location, probably in the basement area, where they would be out of danger from an attack," Duncan replied as he too looked around for signs of activity.

"I doubt they took the elevators, so the stairs then?" she said indicating the door adjacent to the elevator doors.

Duncan simply nodded his agreement.

The two of them approached the door and quietly opened it, listening for any sounds of any activity down there. At the very end sounds of people moving around could just be made out and Duncan closed the door.

"There's someone down there, it sounds like they're coming this way," he said.

"What do you want to do?" she asked, she had her pistol out, so she was all ready to follow his lead.

"We need eyes on them before we commit to anything," he said then taking something from a pouch on his belt, attached it to the barrel of his Walther he then opened the door slightly and fired through the slight gap.

The pistol fired a small device that held several tiny cameras that went flying through the gap and hit the wall in the stairwell. After embedding in the wall, it shot out the tiny cameras which also hit the walls going down the stairwell embedding in the wall where they hit. As soon as this was done, they began to transmit a video feed back to Duncan's PIN.

"Turning to show Sanchez he said, "Now we have eyes on them."

"Cool," she admitted adding, "look, there they are."

The camera feed showed a group of men and women walking up the stairs with rifles raised to their shoulders ready to fire.

"Raine is there behind the first two coming up," Duncan commented when they saw them.

"What are we going to do?" Sanchez asked.

"We need to see what he's done with the virus before we make a move on them."

"Have you got any idea how we can do that?" Sanchez asked.

Duncan looked at her and said, "Not yet, I'm making this up as I go along," he replied.

He opened the door once more and stepped through.

"What the fuck're you doing?" shouted Sanchez, she couldn't believe what she was seeing. Again, he'd acted alone as if she wasn't here with him.

At the top of the stairs Duncan saw the group of four men running up toward him. He took aim and fired at the first man in front dropping him with a head shot. His head exploded backwards covering Raine in his brains. The second man was already moving when he fired again but was hit in the shoulder which spun him around and he went tumbling down the stairs. The two other men had to move to the side to avoid being taken with him. Clearly this was now every man for himself.

Raine wiped blood from his face as he brought his pistol up to fire. The bullet hit the wall near the doorway forcing Duncan to back out that way.

Raine continued to fire as he ran up the last few remaining stairs to burst through the door.

Duncan had retreated to the reception desk taking Sanchez with him. From there they could see anyone coming through the door and remain safe behind the stone reception area.

As they saw the last two of the group burst through the door they had to duck down as the man with Raine blasted his way toward the entrance with his assault rifle on sustained fire. Bullets slammed into the reception dais chipping away at their cover.

"Holy fuck!" Sanchez screamed as she was covered in dust and chips as their cover was systematically destroyed.

The barrage suddenly stopped and slowly the two of them peered over the edge to see the lobby was empty.

"Crap!" Duncan snapped at himself as he realised they had escaped. Getting up he ran to the door and was immediately forced back as a hail of bullets struck the doorframe. Once the shooting stopped, he looked around the corner of the doorjamb and saw two figures getting into a shuttle and taking off. He ran out and fired as fast as his gun would fire at them. He saw his shells impacting on the shuttle's hull with no effect. These craft were built to withstand the rigours of space travel so they were sturdy.

In frustration he had to stand and watch Raine slip through his fingers once more.

"Damn and blast that man," he swore, "he's more slippery than an eel covered in grease."

"What now?" Sanchez asked as she came to his side, "Why was he here anyway?"

Duncan turned to look at her, his frustration once more under control as the problem was running through his mind. What was Raine's intention, why did he come here only to leave shortly after?

He had the virus still, clearly, he had used it already, so what was his purpose in coming here?

Did he bring more of it, and if so, why? He knew the government would hunt him down after his action against the immigration campsites so he must know there would be nowhere left on Altair he could hide; the government would make sure of that. Not if the government was no longer in power though.

"That's it, it had to be," he said finally.

"What's it, what're you talking about?" Sanchez asked as confused as ever.

"He brought some of the virus with him and he left it here to kill off the entire government. We have to get down there and save them," he said.

Chapter 48

Duncan sprinted down the stairs taking them two at a time until he reached the bottom floor. Slamming the door back against the wall he looked around for the Situation Room.

"There," he said to Sanchez at his side.

He tossed a grenade at the door and stepped back inside the stairwell dragging his partner with him.

They felt the blast shake the walls of the corridor and saw the smoke billow out toward where they were hiding.

"Come on," he said and ran toward the room.

As he burst inside, he took a quick look around and saw the crate holding the bomb with the cannister attached.

"Governor, I suggest you remain in here with your men," he said holding his pistol steadily on the rest of the occupants of the room. "The rest of you, grab that crate and let's go," he added.

"Where are you taking it?" Robbins asked.

"As far away from here as we can, giving the time we have left," Duncan told him.

When no one moved Duncan added, "Look, you can all stay here and wait for this thing to go off, that's fine by me, or you can try and help us. Or I could just shoot you now and save me a whole lot of trouble."

Robbins turned to his men and signalled for them to put down their weapons.

"Come on Mykel, there's only two of them, we can take them," one of them argued.

"And do what after? I never planned on dying today, and definitely not here. Marcus left us here to rot, if we die here today, we'll never know if he got what's coming to him," Robbins shot back.

"Oh, I can assure you, he'll get what's coming to him alright," Duncan said.

"Okay, let's give the man a hand then," Robbins said and his men came forward and grabbed hold of the crate hoisting it off the ground. Their faces blanched when they saw the display counting down.

"Where to?" Robbins asked.

"We have to get it upstairs, I have a ship, if we get it on board, I'll fly it up into space and let it blow there where no one will get hurt," Duncan said.

"You heard the man, let's hustle guys," Robbins urged them on.

Raines sat aboard his ship watching the scanner at the front of his control panel. It was displaying the view from below and what was happening at the Council Building.

He was concentrating on the front entrance dividing his attention between the flying controls and the screen.

He knew it wouldn't be long now, a glance at the chronometer told him that they had but minutes left. Those two idiots who came after him, they'd die too.

"One more landing to go," Duncan said quietly as he was mentally counting down the time they had left before this contraption went off. He wasn't sure what exactly was inside that cannister but he figured it was probably the remainder of the Omega Five virus.

At the top he urged them on even more.

"Come on, over to my ship," he said and let them go on ahead. Pulling his partner to one side he said, "You stay back here and keep an eye on them, call for back up then hand them over. I'll be back as soon as I can."

He could tell from her eye roll she thought it was a stupid idea but she said nothing. She obviously couldn't think of an alternative so had decided it best to remain quiet.

As they placed the crate inside Duncan's ship a fleet of vehicles came screeching to a halt near the entrance. Officers from the local security forces poured out, guns raised screaming at everyone to freeze.

Duncan ignored them. "Ship take off immediately, we don't have time to stop and explain what we're doing," he ordered as he entered the bridge.

"Copy that Commander, it could be dangerous for those people too close to us though," the AI informed him.

"Can't be helped Ship. Once they see we're taking off they'll move out of the way, trust me," Duncan said and the ship's engines fired lifting her off the landing pad.

The main engine fired boosting the power and speed taking them up into the air away from the scene below.

Chapter 49

Raine was in orbit waiting to see the fruits of his labour before he took off through to hyperspace and his final destination.

The timer was almost run out when he saw the figures run out of the Council Building. From this height he could just make out that they were carrying something which they loaded onto a starship parked on a landing pad.

A sinking feeling hit his stomach as he knew what was happening and fury built inside him. Slamming his fists down onto the arms of his chair he screamed at the screen in frustration and anger. Once again that wretched agent had thwarted his scheme.

He watched, just to be sure and saw the ship rocket up to the upper atmosphere then jettison something from a hatch and he knew in that moment, he had failed.

"Ship, we need to get far enough out of the atmosphere so that when that thing blows and starts to disperse the virus it doesn't fall back into the atmosphere," Duncan said as he sat in the command chair keeping an eye on the chronometer that was counting down the seconds to detonation.

"Increasing speed to maximum Commander," the AI replied and Duncan felt the main engine kick in boosting their speed.

"How soon Ship?" he asked knowing they were inside the last minute. He saw the sunlight slowly disappear in front of them as they began to leave the atmosphere.

"Jettisoning the package now Commander," the AI informed him.

Duncan altered the viewer to a rear aspect and saw the crate thrust out from the airlock into the darkness of space. It was suddenly lit up brighter than a noon day sun as it exploded in a display of iridescence that dazzled even the stars.

The display was over quickly as the vacuum of outside choked the life from the flames in the blast.

"Were we in time Ship?" Duncan asked almost afraid of the answer in case it was a negative.

"My readings indicate we were successful Commander. The virus was dispersed by the explosion but remained beyond the pull of the planet below and will die out in seconds due to having no host to latch onto," the AI responded.

Duncan sat back in the chair and relaxed for a second.

It had been touch and go whether they would succeed and considering all the lives that were at stake he was glad he could shield his emotions from all of the consequences should they have failed. That was not the case though, and now was the time to celebrate even if it was ever so briefly. Raine had escaped and there was a need to bring him to justice, one way or the other.

He had a deep feeling that this was not over just yet. He had targeted the immigration campsites as the main focus of his anger, but if he knew Raine as well as he suspected he did, then the immigrants weren't the main focus, just the end result of a series of bad decisions.

Those decisions were made by the chain of command, he had already targeted the person responsible for the decision on his homeworld but there was someone higher up the chain who had made the decision before him.

Raine had been desperate to escape the planet and not just to escape the results of what he had put into play here but because he wasn't finished yet. There was one other person on that chain of command who needed to pay for what they had done.

"Ship patch me through to C at MI7," he said. When the call was connected, he said, "Sir, this isn't over yet, Raine is going after the one person he blames for all of this. Increase the security around the President, he's going after him."

Raine set the course for Terra II and made the jump to hyperspace.

He may have failed here but he would not fail again. President Harada would soon feel his wrath and face the consequences of playing with people's lives.

Before he died, he would look him in the eye to let him know who had done this and why.

Chapter 50

New Geneva, Terra II

Raine landed on the roof of the COP Headquarters and left the ship with Sonny Bates, the last of his men.

"Keep the engine prepped, I expect to come out hot," he said as he left the shuttle.

"Copy that," Bates said nervously. He had questioned what Raine was doing coming here and when Raine had told him that it had led to this point, and it would end here, he had no choice but to go along with it. After all, where else could he go?

As with every building that had a landing pad on the roof, there was access to the building inside which Raine walked to, nonchalantly. The door was secured and he was in a hurry so he didn't take the time to unlock it he simply affixed an explosive charge to the lock, small but effective and stood around the corner of the stairway. The explosion was muted due to the shape of the charge, it had been designed to direct all the energy from the blast onto the lock destroying it and little else around it.

Once it was open, he went through the door and down the stairwell to the top floor of the building.

As Duncan arrived over the COP Headquarters, he spotted the shuttle parked on one of the landing pads on the rooftop.

"Ship, is that the shuttle Raine took off in, if so, disable it," he said.

Without needing to respond the ship fired a rocket at the engine section of the shuttle below. The explosion ripped the rear section apart lifting it off the ground. It slammed back down skewed across the landing pad still smoking from the blast with wreckage littering the ground around it.

Bates saw the other ship come in toward the rooftop at speed. He was about to contact Raine to inform him they had company when he saw the rocket fired at him.

With nowhere to go he simply braced himself and prayed he would survive.

The rocket struck the rear section of the shuttle destroying the engine and their last chance of getting off this roof alive. He felt the heat from the blast hit him on his back as the shuttle was lifted of the ground to be slammed down a moment later.

Already shaken from the explosion Bates was stunned by the impact with the ground. As the shuttle settled, he felt darkness overwhelm him and his last thought was he hoped Raine had a plan for this.

———

"Good work," Duncan said in admiration, "now get me down there."

Under the AI's control, the ship swooped down faster than a human could handle and placed it on another landing pad at the opposite end from the burning shuttle. Duncan was out of his seat and at the hatch the instant they were down.

Running down the ramp he had his pistol drawn as he went after Raine. He saw the door lock to the stairwell had been destroyed so he went through the door and into the brightly lit stairwell.

Listening for sounds of activity Duncan continued down the stone stairs aware that he could run into his target at any second.

The Council Chambers would be on one of the lower floors, possibly even the basement. There was no way of knowing where the President would be at this time. If he was aware of the danger then he would be in the bunker deep in the basement.

"Where would Raine go first?" he thought as he descended onto the top floor of the building. Harada's office was up here somewhere but surely, he must have been informed of the attack on Altair.

Seeing no one around he assumed the alarm had been sounded and everyone had departed to a safer location, that included the President.

Searching for the fastest way down to the bunker he spotted the elevator at the far end of the corridor he was in.

Once he was inside, he punched the button for the basement level.

Raine looked around the top floor searching for any sign of activity when he heard the explosion on the roof.

They had found him. He thought he'd arrived before they would have figured out his destination and intentions, that was obviously not the case.

He had underestimated them, again. They were beginning to become more than just an annoyance. Now they were a direct threat to the success of his plans. Not to worry though, this had always been a possibility and he had planned for it.

Every tall building had measures built into it in case of emergency, whether it was a fire, structural damage or a terrorist attack. There had to be a way of getting those people in the upper floors away to safety. A system of fire prevention methods was included in any plans for any building over seven floors tall as after that fire teams from the ground could not attack it. Escape methods were also built into taller buildings these usually included a way of escaping the top floors safely.

Raine searched for this buildings escape route. There was a time when fire officials recommended that anyone caught in a fire in a high-rise building remain where they were and wait for the firemen to arrive and rescue you. Nowadays it was easier and faster to use the escape systems.

In this building, the system was a fire-retardant chute that extended from every floor and went down the side of the building. Raine activated the system which was in the wall of the President's office on this floor. Obviously, he would be the first to evacuate in any dangerous situation so he knew where the system would be. The hatch opened in the wall and the chute extended out from the building. Grabbing the hand rail inside the hatch he swung his legs up and into the chute then allowed gravity to do the rest.

Once inside the chute he sped down toward the ground slowed by a system of buffeting air cushions operated from the ground below which gave him a soft landing.

The entire journey from the office to the ground was completed in seconds and when he landed, he walked away from the building, just another pedestrian going about his business leaving onlookers wondering what had just happened.

Chapter 51

Duncan ran across the rooftop as soon as the ship landed. Going through the door that Raine had left open he ran down the stairs to the top floor of the building.

Where was he?

Seeing no sign of him he ran to the President's office. Bursting through the door he had his SAP10 out scanning the room for hostiles.

Nothing.

There was no sign of Raine or the President.

He couldn't waste any time searching the building, he had to choose the best option and go there right away and then he saw it.

Over by the far wall, the escape chute had been activated.

Was this a ruse, a diversion to take him away from the real objective? How could he be certain?

Moving to the President's desk he used his PIN to log in to the computer. Once he had access, he asked for the location of the President. The result showed Harada was safely guarded down in the basement in the bunker.

Logging off he replaced his PIN in his pouch and went after Raine.

He threw himself down the chute feet first feeling the rush of air as he soon reached terminal velocity and then the cushioning kicked in slowing his descent.

When he got to the end of the tunnel he landed on his feet and looked around.

Bystanders stared at him aghast that a second man had emerged from the chute.

Looking around the area all he could see was a sea of faces, some staring at him whilst others ignored him. Locating Raine through this ocean was proving impossible. He had nothing to go on, no tracker available to him, no options left to him.

Raine had gotten away, again.

Having business ventures all over his homeworld it wasn't difficult for Raine to find somewhere to hide or a mode of transport to utilise on any other planet.

A short walk from the building took Raine to a transport terminal that supplied various modes of transport to everyone whether it was by rail, bus or a shuttle to a ship in orbit waiting to take them off world.

Raine chose a self-drive shuttle that was available and took off changing his destination mid-flight. These shuttles had pre-destined flights to various locations where other customers would be waiting to use them. Raine disabled the location tracker and the computer overdrive which meant he had total manual control and the base couldn't wrest control of him when he veered off course to bring him either back or take him to the nearest base whichever was easiest.

Being blind to their scanners he was free to go wherever he wanted.

Setting course for the coast he set off for his new and final destination.

Duncan returned to his ship took his seat in the command chair.

"Ship, patch me in to C at HQ," he said.

"Give me your progress Pryde," Chambers said hopefully.

"Sir the President is safe but unfortunately Raine escaped. I have no idea at this moment where he has gone,"

"In that case we'll have to pick up his trail another time. Report back to base for your debrief, perhaps we can learn something from it if we look at it from a different perspective."

"Copy that sir, I'm on my way," Duncan said then added, "Ship take us back to base."

"Copy that Commander," the AI said and took the ship into the air.

As the ship rose and flew over the city's buildings Duncan sat going over everything in his mind. What could he have done better to bring this to an absolute conclusion?

At every turn Raine had been one step ahead of him. He had come close a couple of times but whenever that happened, it seemed Raine had a plan for it. He had said earlier that it was a game of chess and so far they had been at least one move behind him all the way.

If he wanted to end this then capturing Raine might not be an option, he may have to come up withing a little more permanent. He didn't have a problem with that, he did wonder how he might get close enough to fulfil that part of the mission though.

It was going to be difficult; they had no idea where he might go, what he might do next or when. His main objective of bringing the President to task over the latest population sanctions seemed to have been a failure so what did he plan to do next?

If they wanted to get a step ahead, they would have to anticipate his next move. It might help if they had a clue as to what he might be thinking.

As he sat there thinking, he saw the headquarters building approaching and something occurred to him.

Chapter 52

Raine poured himself a stiff measure of Santuro Whiskey, a thirty-year single malt distilled on Altair and one of his favourites, into a crystal tumbler then threw in three large ice cubes.

Sitting down in the chair on the veranda that overlooked the coastline from the clifftop he looked out over the seas breaking on the shore and remarked to himself on how this view was never going to be as wonderful as those back on Altair. He was tired but he was also angry. All his hard work seemed to have come to a full stop, for the moment at least.

This too, was part of the plan, but it was a part he'd hoped he wouldn't have had to consider though. Now he was here, away from it all waiting for the dust to settle before getting back to it and finishing off what he had started. They would assume he had returned to Altair and never think to look right under their noses.

It would end only one way now; of that he was certain. He was determined to see it through now to the bitter end.

No one knew of this villa he had on the south coast, it had been his little secret for years, his little bolt hole should the need arise where he had to get off Altair for whatever reason.

There was never any staff here so he had to get used to doing things for himself. He'd cooked himself a meal and was now relaxing as he watched the sun set over the horizon.

His thoughts turned once more to his prime target. When he achieved this final act, he would have to do it in a way that protected his freedom. It would be tricky but he knew he could pull it off.

All he had to do was wait and all the pieces would fall into place.

Chapter 53

Mi7 Hq

Duncan was back at headquarters ready to see C in his office when he heard a voice he recognised.

"Thanks for coming back for me," it said. He turned to see Sanchez standing there he could see she was angry by how her hands rested on her hips and her lips firmly pressed together.

"I didn't," he said simply then looked away as if the conversation was finished.

"He'll see you now Duncan, you too Agent Sanchez," Goodchild said.

"Thank you," Sanchez said giving her a smile at the use of Duncan's first name.

The two of them entered the office and took the two chairs placed in front of the table.

"Now then, Agent Pryde, how did you manage to let Raine get away from you?" C asked as they sat down in front of him.

"I didn't allow him to do anything sir, he escaped before I had arrived. I searched for him but there was no sign of him."

"What do you intend on doing now then?" C asked.

"Everything I can to find him and stop him sir," Duncan said coldly.

"You might have to accept that this one may have gotten away from us."

"I'm sorry sir, I can't do that. I will find him and he will face justice, sir. That you can be certain of."

"Don't make promises you can't keep," C told him.

"I haven't sir," he replied with a straight face. He gave a slight head tilt, a sign of his confusion at why he would even suggest that.

"Quite, anyway, there are steps being taken to protect the President in future. For the short term he will be moved to a secure location while we try to put an end to this debacle," C said.

Duncan nodded as he listened to what was being said. C continued with, "You look like hell. I think you should take time to recover, take a few days off and get your strength back. I'll keep you informed if we learn anything new."

"Thank you, sir, but I'd rather remain on duty so I can react immediately something new turns up," he replied.

"Don't make me make it an order Duncan, get out of here and I don't want to see you for at least three days. Get some sleep at least and some food and then come back when you've recovered enough to do the job."

Duncan knew there was nothing to be gained from him arguing with him over this so he simply nodded his agreement and got to his feet to leave.

"You too Agent Sanchez, you could do with some rest too," C added.

"You won't get an argument from me sir," she replied and was on her feet straight away heading for the door.

As Duncan left the office there was something nagging at him at the back of his mind. Something he'd missed and he couldn't quite put his finger on it.

Probing his mind would do no good at this point for the further he probed, the deeper he tried to go, the more it retreated from his grasp.

His mind was fatigued which was the problem so maybe taking C's advice might help after all. He decided to go home and try and rest for a few hours. Hopefully when he woke, the problem he was searching for an answer to might surface enough for him to grab it.

He had an idea that it could be the solution he was searching for and no matter how hard he searched for it, in his condition he would never find it.

Grabbing his car, he drove home to his apartment. He went straight inside and to his bedroom. He dropped onto the King-sized bed and was asleep in seconds.

Chapter 54

Cop Hq

President Harada woke the next day after a troubled night's sleep.

He had come close to being the target of Marcus Raine, a man capable and determined and who had made him the focus of his campaign of hatred and xenophobia.

Being a career politician, he seldom contemplated the effects of his policies on the little people until today. He had seen the effects in the thousands of deaths Raine had perpetrated in the twelve immigration campsites. The actual number of dead still had to be confirmed but it was in the tens of thousands and reports were coming in from various social media platforms that were arguing that he was to blame for the actions taken by Raine.

This could turn into career ending if he didn't get a hold of it before it got too big to handle. He had to get his narrative out to the public before they got too invested in this other one.

"We are ready to move you Mister President sir," General Aslam said. He was the head of the Coalition Defence Force and had taken the President's security personally.

"I'm ready," Harada replied. He had eaten breakfast and was prepared, everything he needed would be at the new location. He knew it wouldn't be for long and it had to be done to ensure his safety, but that didn't mean he had to like it.

The two of them left the room to be greeted outside the door by a phalanx of armed security guards. They all wore the obligatory black suits with tell-tale bulges under their jackets denoting where their SAP10's were holstered.

They escorted the President out of the building through a hidden exit into a shuttle that had an escort of its own. Two Marauder F75 fighter jets were already in the air circling the area above the headquarters building to ensure their flight path was clear.

Under the careful scrutiny of the two F75's the shuttle took off and flew up above the city's landscape where the F 75's took up their position, one on either side.

In a few seconds they were over the city leaving the restricted airspace.

Chapter 55

Mi7 Hq

Duncan returned to SecOps once he'd had a shower and a change of clothes.

He still felt tired from the previous ordeals and the thought he hadn't quite managed to bring to the forefront of his mind still lurked somewhere at the back.

It was irritating and frustrating how it prodded and tickled but wouldn't quite come near enough for him to realise what it was. He'd put it down to his brain being tired but clearly, that wasn't the entirety of it. He had slept, albeit fitfully, but he had slept, so why couldn't he grasp what it was that was eluding him?

"Good morning Duncan, nice to see you looking relaxed," Goodchild said as he neared her station outside C's office.

"I don't feel rested," he replied abruptly. She must have seen his brow furrow as he was deep in thought because she asked, "What is it, what's bothering you?"

"If I knew that, it wouldn't be bothering me," he replied.

"Ah, one of those."

"What do you mean?" he asked with a head tilt of confusion.

"There's something tickling you at the back of your mind, but you can't quite grasp it? One of those," she explained.

He smiled a little, "Glad I'm not the only one then," he said.

"No Duncan, most people experience something like this at some point. It's called being human."

He looked at her, the sides of his mouth turning down in indignation.

"I'm human," he said as if to point out the fallacy of her point.

"Yes dear, you carry on believing that and one day it might even come true," she said with a smile and nod of her head.

Not knowing how to respond to that he just turned away and headed towards C's office.

"Come in Pryde, I hope you got some sleep last night?" C said as he entered. Sitting in front of the desk was Agent Sanchez, a fact that caused a confused frown to cross his brow.

"Somewhat sir, thanks. Did I miss something, did you send out a call to the office?" he asked as he sat next to his partner.

"No, Agent Sanchez arrived just before you did."

"Has there been any word about Raine, sir?" Duncan asked.

"Nothing yet, I'm sure he'll pop up soon enough. In the meantime, the President is being moved to a new, safer location until all of this has been settled. We can't have people running around trying to kill him now, can we?" C said.

Duncan was quiet for a second. Something stirred at the back of his mind, creeping slowly into the light. He could almost see it.

"What is it, you look like you're going to be sick?" Sanchez said when she saw his expression.

"Shut up," he snapped at her holding a hand up to stem further comments from her.

Concentrating fully on this thread he finally grasped it, just a little then carefully, began to reel it in. The closer it got, the clearer it all became until enough was visible and he had it.

"Holy shit! Why didn't I see it from the start?" he said.

"What is it man, spit it out," C demanded.

Duncan looked up at his boss and actually smiled.

"Sir, I know where Raine is," he said in triumph.

Chapter 56

The President's convoy over the coast

"How long before we arrive at the new quarters?" Harada asked. He was sitting in the shuttle surrounded by security guards all vigilant and prepared for whatever might be thrown at them.

"Not long now, Mister President. We'll be coming in over the residence in a few more minutes," replied Derek Bannister, the Agent in charge of this detail.

"I hope so, I have too much work to be done to waste time like this," Harada moaned, he was grumpy at having his routine rescheduled without his say so. He liked to be in control but this was one of those rare occasions where he had to relinquish that control in favour of the Secret Service who were in charge of his security. "What about the Cabinet, will they be there too?" he added.

"You'll be able to conference call them sir, our main priority now, is your safety. Let us do our jobs sir," Bannister said. He was becoming more irritated at his constant complaining which was making him sound more like the entitled brat he was. This was a side the public never got to see. They only got to see the regal statesman, a thinly disguised veneer that quickly crumbled under pressure especially behind closed doors.

Bannister had no doubt of his political credentials, he could do the job, there was never any doubt about that, his motives on the other hand, there was plenty of doubt there. He was in this for the status and what could be earned from it, and nothing more. He never had any feelings for the common people he was elected to represent, their only job was to vote him into office, when that was done, he couldn't care less what happened to them.

"I suppose so," he replied sullenly. All this did concern him, especially when things happened that made him look bad, such as the recent deaths of those immigrants. He had a team working on a new spin of the story. It was caused by a deranged terrorist who had a grudge against off-worlders and had targeted them. He was to be presented as a magnanimous benefactor allocating space on a world to those who were homeless through no fault of their own. He had done everything in his power to ensure their safety and a new start on a new world.

By the time his team were done he would come out of it looking like a new messiah.

"Approaching landing site now sir," the pilot announced over the intercom system.

Harada sighed briefly as the journey was finally coming to an end and he could get back to work.

Sitting in a large ATV with a hand-picked team, Kaufman watched the convoy approach from above.

They had taken up position on the coast, close to, but not within range of the residence's sensors to avoid detection.

When he saw the convoy come within range he simply said, "Fire."

The target lock chime made the pilot of one of the F75's look at his screens. So far, the flight had been uneventful. Now though things were about to heat up.

"Incoming," he said into the radio to inform the convoy before taking evasive manoeuvres. He moved the control stick over to the left to veer away from the shuttle and take the missile fired at him with him.

He was too late though, seeing the warning too late as the engine behind him blew up in a fireball that quickly engulfed the entire fighter jet. He never even had time to eject. He was dead shortly after issuing his warning.

The second flanking aircraft fared no better. The missile fired at him was released simultaneously as the other and as he watched his partner explode, he didn't have time to react before he was torn apart by a massive explosion.

Splash two fighter jets. The President's shuttle was alone.

The explosions lit up the inside of the shuttle like a firework display on the Fourth of July on Earth.

"What the fuck just happened?" Harada asked already fearing the worst. He felt his stomach cramp in panic as fear took hold of him.

"We just lost our escort," Bannister said. Into his comm link he said, "Get back up in the air right now. Secure the landing zone, we're coming in hot."

Before any acknowledgement could be received, the passengers in the shuttle felt the entire craft shoved from behind, like a giant hand had just reached out and pushed them forward.

"What's happening now?" Harada screamed looking around in panic. His breathing quickened up from his fear and his eyes widened.

"We sustained a hit to our rear," Bannister explained. He placed a firm hand on the President's chest pushing him back in his seat.

"It'll be best if you remained seated sir. I'm sure the pilot has everything under control," he said keeping his voice as calm and soothing as he could.

"We just lost engine control, we're going down," the pilot said through the Intership comms.

Harada looked into Bannister's eyes; his lips firmly pressed together in anger.

"Under control?" he said.

Chapter 57

K aufman smiled when he saw the two fighters go down.

Phase one completed.

On to phase two.

"Move in and take control of the shoreline," he said to the men sitting out beyond the sight line of the white sandy beaches on this stretch of coastline.

The cruiser he had as part of his militia had dropped anchor off shore and stood ready to supply whatever was needed for this phase of the operation. It was the ship they had all arrived in and was just as capable of being sea worthy as it was space worthy.

Three landing craft emerged from a hatch in the starboard hull and quickly sped away heading for the beach. Each craft held more than thirty members of Kaufman's militia and each man or woman was armed ready for battle.

The shuttle carrying the President and his security detail headed for the ground, their trail was easily traced by the smoke trailing from the damaged rear section.

Kaufman didn't much care either way if he lived or died, he was doing his part by securing the beach and removing the air cover on the ariel convoy. He was only there to give ground support; the rest would be up to Raine.

A jet copter appeared over the shoreline near where he was parked and troops began to rappel down to the ground then spread out to make sure the area was covered and no one would get in or out.

He got out of the vehicle to survey his people's work and from his vantage point overlooking both the road and the beach area he could see everything, including the supposed residence where the President was going.

He contacted Raine and said, "The area is secure and Presidential One is down."

"Stand fast, I'm coming in," replied Raine and Kaufman smiled that cruel smile that said someone was going to get hurt soon, really bad.

Harada was still strapped into his seat, shaken but okay. The landing was better than he had expected.

Instead of crashing, the pilot had managed to bring her down in a controlled descent using thrusters only to reduce speed then make the touch down as gentle as possible.

After bouncing a few times when he thought his teeth had been rattled free, they stopped at the end of a sliding spin in the middle of a road that led to their final destination.

Bannister said, "Right people, everyone grab as much as you can and make your way towards the residence. Mister President, you stay with me at all times."

Harada nodded his agreement; he wasn't about to argue about anything here. He was more than willing to leave this to the experts. Pain shot through his shoulder as he unclamped the harness holding him place, which had undoubtedly saved him from further harm. He must have jarred it during the landing as it hurt like hell. Saying nothing he got out of the seat noticing other aches and pains but decided to try and ignore them until they were better suited to examine them, when they had reached safety perhaps.

All around him the men and women in his security detail were checking weapons and had the steely look of a soldier about to go into battle, one that he knew he would not survive.

He didn't know whether to be proud or terrified. After realising what it meant to go into battle, terror won out.

Shaking from head to foot, Harada followed instructions from Bannister and they left the damaged wreck of the shuttle.

He looked around and saw the troops falling from the chopper then turned to glance toward the beach shoreline and saw more troops, and his fear came to the front.

"How the fuck are we getting out of here alive?" he hissed through clenched teeth.

"We will do whatever is necessary to keep you safe Mister President," Bannister replied calmly. He was crouching down by the side of the shuttle also surveying the area. "If I were you sir, I would get down lower so you don't present such an inviting target," he added.

"Are you saying they're here to kill me?" Harada said as if only just realising what was going on.

"You *were* in the shuttle with us that they shot down sir," he replied thinking that at times it was like talking to a twelve-year-old kid.

"Keep close to me sir, do everything I tell you and you will get out of this alive," Bannister said.

Harada nodded and the stern look in Bannister's eyes told him not to argue.

Chapter 58

Mi7 Hq

"What do you mean, you know where he is?" C asked.

"Well not exactly, at least not until we learn where President Harada is being taken," Duncan said.

"You think he's going to make another play for him, don't you?" Sanchez said.

"It's the only thing that makes sense," he replied.

C immediately got onto the intercom and called Goodchild, "Get me the whereabouts of the President immediately," he said.

"I'm on it, sir," she replied.

"You two, get moving. I'll send you the location as soon as I get it. I'll have a tac team ready to move to your location as soon as you get confirmation," C said with a wave to send them on their way.

Duncan got up and headed for the door. He felt rejuvenated, he had a target once more, something to focus his energy on.

Sanchez was with him running from the office.

"Ship, get prepped, we're taking off as soon as we arrive. You'll have the destination by the time we get there," Duncan said through his comms.

They reached the landing pad and ran up the ramp to get inside the ship.

"Welcome aboard Commander and Agent Sanchez, glad to have you back," the AI said as they entered the bridge and took their seats. "I have the co-ordinates already sent to your PIN, they are laid in and are available at your command sir," it added.

"Okay, Ship, let's get going then," Duncan said.

The safe house was less than a hundred metres from where they went down but as Bannister judged their situation it might as well be a few hundred miles.

They were cut off from it, the only cover available was the shuttle. Troops were lining the beach area cutting off any escape that way and up on the roadside area was another line of troops forming a barrier between them and the safe house.

Assessing their chances of reaching it Bannister concluded they were fucked. He wasn't about to tell Harada that though, a panicked president was the last thing he needed right now.

He'd tried to call in for reinforcements but their comm lines were being jammed.

His options were running out very quickly and pretty soon Harada was going to ask, again, how they were going to get out of this and he had nothing of value to say to him.

"Mister President, by now you have reached the conclusion that there is no way out of this without further bloodshed. If you don't want any of that shed blood to be yours then I suggest you follow my orders to the letter," a voice boomed out through an electronic amplifying device.

Bannister looked at Harada whose expression had suddenly become hopeful. They were offering him a way out of this where he would live, and he was seriously considering taking it.

Harada was about to reply when Bannister clamped a hand over the president's mouth.

"You will say nothing, sir," he said.

Harada grabbed the hand and tore it from his mouth before shouting, "What do you want me to do?"

"That was fast, no attempt to bargain with us, no delaying tactics, I'm impressed, it seems the rumours about you being a cowardly narcissist are all true. I especially like how you asked what I want you to do and not all of you, it gives more of a perspective on what your character is really like," the voice replied.

Bannister sneered at Harada, unable to keep the contempt from turning the sides of his mouth down. "You just sold us all out. He now knows you'll do anything to save your own skin, even if it means we die," he said.

"Truth be told Agent, whatever your name is, I am more important than you are. I am the President of the Coalition

Of Planets, who are you again?" Harada said with equal contempt.

"I'm the man trying to keep you alive, you ungrateful fuck," Bannister said ignoring protocol of always addressing him by his title.

"Well, it seems I can do that on my own," Harada said and stood up from behind the shuttle. He stood proud, his hands on his hips and his head held high so they could all see him in his splendour.

As he began to walk away toward the road Bannister looked around at what was left of his detail and they all wore the same contempt on their faces he felt, and something else, the realisation that without Harada there, there was no reason to keep them alive.

A silent command was given and the troops along the beach opened fire on the shuttle.

A hailstorm of bullets and rocket propelled grenades struck the downed shuttle destroying it along with the men using it for cover, in a display of violence rarely seen along that stretch of coastline.

Harada flinched, crouching down the moment the shooting started but Kaufman assured him he was safe, "Don't worry Mister President, my men are all expert marksmen, you will not be harmed. We have no need of your security detail now anyway, they would just be an extra encumbrance, better to dispose of them now," he said.

Without a second thought, Harada continued up toward the roadside where a group of armed men were waiting for his arrival.

The way he strutted up to them gave them the impression he thought he was in control because they wanted him alive. An impression that was quickly dispelled when the nearest man struck him in the face with the butt of his rifle knocking him clean out along with three of his teeth.

Kaufman walked up to stand over the fallen figure and he spat on it in contempt.

"I hate cowards," he said.

Turning to walk away he said, "Drag that piece of shit to the truck, we're leaving."

Chapter 59

"Down there," Sanchez said indicating the wreckage of the shuttle that had carried the President and his security detail.

"Take us down Ship, put us as close to that shuttle as possible," Duncan said.

"Copy that Commander."

The ship landed on the road and the two agents debarked with their pistols drawn ready to fight. The ran down to the shuttle wreckage and started looking around. Bodies were flung around from explosions while others lay near the wreckage, shot to pieces.

"Whatever happened here, it was brutal," Sanchez commented as she wandered around examining the site.

"There's no sign of the President or his body, which means either he escaped, or they took him hostage," Duncan said.

"Can you imagine him escaping this?" Sanchez asked.

"Correct, so it seems obvious now that he was taken from here by the perpetrators," Duncan agreed having come to the same conclusion himself.

"Do you still think Raine is behind this?" she asked.

"I do, he was in the perfect place to pull something like this off. He was the owner of a munitions business that supplied to this world's military, he had an abundance of personnel and we know he escaped his last attempt on the President's life."

"Didn't C say that all his assets had been sequestered though, wouldn't that put a damper on his being able to fund something like this?"

Duncan thought about that, his brow creased in thought. It was a valid point she made which he may have overlooked and then the solution occurred to him.

"You're right but when you did research on Kaufman and his militia, didn't you say he had followers of up to a thousand men and women?"

"That's correct."

"We didn't see anywhere close to that number when we invaded his compound, not did we see any sign of the man himself. What if he had taken the bulk of his forces to prepare for this phase of the operation?"

"I see where you're going with this, it would explain why we only saw a fraction of his militia at the compound and also why we never saw Kaufman."

"Those tracks on the beach there," he said indicated the footsteps and deep groves in the sand where the landing craft came ashore, "looks to me like they made a beach landing from somewhere off shore to cut off any retreat this way. They obviously brought down the shuttle after taking care of the air support, probably from down here somewhere with a surface to air missile. They'd cut off their retreat into the water, then they made it impossible for them to reach the residence. I'm not quite sure how they got the President but once they had it was clear they had no further need of his detail, so they eliminated them with extreme prejudice."

Nodding her head to agree with his assessment of the situation as she looked around, she turned to him to ask, "So where do you think they took him?"

"I have no clue but maybe we can find out," he replied. "Ship access the satellite feeds covering this section of the coastline. Scan for anything arriving and then leaving this specific area within the last hour," he said through the link to the ship.

"Copy that Commander," came the reply. Within seconds the AI had accessed the satellite feed but had also recognised what they needed.

"Commander, I have a group of vehicles arriving by land on the road close to the residence with a cruiser arriving off shore. Several landing craft left the anchored cruiser to form a line across the beach. Up on the road the convoy of vehicles shot down the air support fighter jets then downed the shuttle. President Harada left his detail to walk up to the vehicles on the road just before the detail were attacked from both angles. The detail was clinically destroyed between a crossfire that used both small arms fire and rocket propelled grenades. Sir, they would have had little chance of survival."

"What happened to the President? Where did they take him?" Duncan asked.

"As soon as he reached the road, they rendered him unconscious then placed him on board one of the ATV's and drove off sir."

"Is that it? Do you have a direction at least to where they went?

"I assumed you would need that information as well Commander so I expanded my search using other satellites. I have a location for you sir, but you may not like it," the AI said.

Duncan looked at Sanchez and they both had the same expression that said 'what else can go wrong'.

"Tell me," Duncan said.

Chapter 60

"The Kamino station, really? That's where they took him?" C said when Duncan contacted him.

"Yes sir, we tracked the vehicles who took him to a landing pad near the safe house just up the coast where they transferred him to a shuttle that took him up to the station," explained Duncan.

"How did they get access to it, I thought it was being run by a private company?"

"It seems he has assets within the holding company that owns the station. Apparently, sir, Raine is the owner."

"This can't be good. I can't send troops up to a privately owned station without good cause," C said.

"Leave it to us sir, we'll get the proof you need to send in the troops. Give us a few hours and we'll give you a sit rep once we get aboard the station and assess the situation," Duncan suggested.

"You have one hour before I have to hand it over to the CDF. When that happens, they will no doubt send in a full attack squad so you better work fast," C informed him.

"Copy that sir, we're on our way," Duncan replied then ended the call.

Sanchez was looking at him smiling.

"What?" he asked.

"That's the first time you said 'we' when talking about this op. All the other times it's been 'you'," she replied.

"Come on, we have a job to do, and only an hour to get it done in," he said ignoring her comment.

Chapter 61

High up in orbit around Terra II the Kamino Station was a privately owned communications station.

Owned by one of Marcus Raine's subsidiary companies in his corporation it was the largest communication station ever seen.

Twenty-five decks and the size of a football field it was a massive structure kept in place by its fusion drive. Able to monitor every single communication on the planet it was used to channel comms for the Coalition.

No military personnel were on board, it had been a stipulation of the contract that they would give access to the comms to the Coalition as long as they were allowed to run it independently with no oversight from the government. It had been a hard bargain but one Harada was willing to concede at the time. It gave everyone concerned what they wanted. For the company who owned the station it gave them the freedom they required to expand their market and for the government it gave them access to all the comm on, and around the planet.

When Harada was brought on board by Kaufman and his men it was the first time, he had set foot on the station. The fear he tried to keep under control prevented him from enjoying the spectacle of what this station was and what it represented.

The main control deck was where all the comms were routed and monitored through. It was a circular area with monitors showing various views positioned around the wall. A huge reinforced window gave a spectacular view of the planet below and the space beyond. The vista of stars twinkling like candles seen through holes in an inky black blanket was breath-taking and gave a sudden perspective of how small and inconsequential our lives are in the enormity of the galaxy.

Harada stopped as he saw the view, for the first time taking it all in and then saw the room around him and for the first time since the attack on him begun he forgot the danger he was in.

"Welcome aboard my little project Mister President," Raine said getting up from a command chair positioned in the centre of the huge room.

"Why have you brought me here?" Harada asked when he saw him.

"Straight to the point, I like that, although it's not your style, is it? As a politician you usually spend a few minutes beating about the bush, telling people what your administration has done for them before not answering any questions put to you. I must say, I find this rather refreshing," Raine said with a smile.

"Is there a point that you're circling around to at any time, which would be nice because I have things to attend to," Harada said feeling his confidence returning a little.

Shaking his head slowly as if admonishing a small boy he said, "I'm afraid you're going to have to put those things on hold for, well, indefinitely actually," he said.

Harada looked at him, then looked around at those men who had brought him to this place and his fear returned in all its glory. "What do you want from me?" he asked his voice showing signs of his anxiety from the way it trembled slightly.

Raine stepped up to him and with a broad, yet cruel smile, said, "Now we're getting somewhere, finally you're asking the right question."

Looking into his cold eyes Harada knew that whatever he was about to say it wasn't going to be good.

Chapter 62

"Ship, how close can you get us to that station without us being detected?" Duncan asked. Him and Sanchez were seated on the bridge looking out over the vast expanse. They had stopped on the very edge of the station's sensor range.

"This is as far as I can go Commander. From here on here you and Agent Sanchez will have to go wearing your EVA suits with the camo-shields," the AI replied.

"Okay, let's go," he said turning to Sanchez. "Are you up for this?" he asked.

"You mean, facing a large group of Neo-Nazi's as well as a madman who blames the President for ruining his world all the time trying to rescue the same President? Do I have a choice?" she replied.

"Of course, you have a choice. We all have choices, you can choose to remain here or come with me, your choice," he said.

"Well, I certainly can't let you do this alone."

"That is your choice."

"Not really, we are partners, or did you forget that?"

"I am trying to," he said with a head tilt, "but you're right, on this op, we are partners so I think we best get going."

"I have the EVA suits prepped for you along with what weapons you might need for this mission," the AI said breaking the tension between them.

"Thanks Ship, keep a lock on us, we might need a fast evac," Duncan said as he left the bridge.

"You see your planet below us, Terra II? I'm going to make you watch as I do to that planet what you did to mine," Raine said.

"What did I do to your world?" Harada asked confusion bringing his eyebrows down over his eyes.

"You took control away from us. You allowed a number of refugees to be placed on Altair placing our whole ecological system in jeopardy. You did this without a second thought to the consequences of your actions because it was never going to impact your own life. Now you are about to see what it is like to have all of that happen to your home and to have no control over it."

"What was I supposed to do, allow those people to die? Something had to be done and I chose your world because it was the closest system that could accommodate them."

"But we couldn't accommodate them, not in the long term, and you and your advisors should have taken all of that into consideration."

"So, slaughtering them all, that was your solution?" Harada asked.

"Just as you made a choice to save lives, I made a choice to sacrifice those same lives to save millions more," Raine told him. He had no sign of apologising for what he had done. In his mind he had done the right thing, just as Harada had thought he was doing when he made his decision.

"You are insane, you know that, don't you?" Harada said.

"Am I? You may be right. The definition of insanity is performing the same thing over and over with the expectation of a different out come each time. According to that I may be insane as I kept hoping you would come to your senses and see the harm you were doing to my world. Every time you made a decision for us, I thought maybe this time they'll get it right and yet here we are."

Harada tried a different tack.

"Okay so you say every time I made a decision you hoped for a different outcome. What if I promise you a different outcome this time? What if I promise to get it right, this time, right now? I have the power to make all this go away and your record be cleansed. I can do that," he said.

"How?" Raine asked staring at him with even more contempt. Now he was begging for his life, a step he expected him to take.

"I can guarantee you autonomy for your own world. I can ensure you make your own decisions from now on, make your own trade deals and so forth. As long as you release me,

I can do all that and, in a few weeks, as soon as the measures are in place Altair will be a truly self-governing world."

"What if I refuse?" Raine asked.

"If you continue on this path, the CDF will attack this station and release me but I cannot testify to what they'll do to you or the people working here. It's your choice Marcus, I pray you'll make the right one," Harada told him wishing he felt as confident as he sounded.

Raine made the pretence of actually mulling it over. He turned away walking a few paces from him then back again and when he looked at the president's expectant expression, he couldn't help but break out in laughter.

"You actually thought I'd go for that didn't you?" he said his laughter exploding from him.

Harada looked at him his brow furrowing in confusion, he had no clue what was happening here.

"Marcus, you have little choice here, the CDF will come for me. We have a policy never to negotiate with terrorists," he pleaded.

"I'm no terrorist, I'm a patriot and who said anything about negotiating?" Raine said finally getting his laughter under control.

"So, what is this about exactly, if you don't want anything, why have you brought me here?"

"I already told you, you are about to face what we faced on Altair. I am going to destroy your world, oh not as slowly as you would have done to mine, but it will be destroyed none the less. As this happens you will have to watch it unfold unable to do anything to prevent it or even warn them of what is coming. Then you'll know what it's like to have control of your own destiny taken from you."

Harada knew then there was no point in arguing, debating or even trying to convince him he was on the path to his own destruction. He was hell bent on completing what he had set out to do and was not about to be diverted from that path.

He was screwed, everyone would remember this as being the day President Harada did nothing to prevent a catastrophe that caused millions of lives. His legacy forever would be tainted. His name would always be linked to this one incident.

Raine saw his expression and knew what was running through his mind.

"You're thinking how this is going to affect you aren't you? How people will remember you in the future and not one single thought about the people who are about to die. Wow, that is some serious narcissism right there. Well just think on that then, just think how people will feel about the president who sat by and watched his people die and did nothing. Not even you will be able to spin this into something favourable for you."

Harada couldn't hole his gaze because he knew he was right, and finally he dropped his eyes to the floor, not in shame but in fear. Fear that he would live through this and have to face the consequences of what happened here today. To his, that was more unbearable to face than watching millions of people die.

Chapter 63

Coalition HQ

General Aslam sat at his desk reviewing the reports from the attack on the President's convoy.

"What do we know?" he asked his aide.

"We have reports from the Ministry that say the President has been taken to the Kamino station in orbit sir."

"Are these reports confirmed?"

"Not as yet sir."

"What other options have we got? What about surveillance footage of the attack, what has that brought up?"

"It shows the attack and the President being taken away while the shuttle he was in, along with his entire detail, destroyed. It then shows the vehicles travelling to a landing pad where they all boarded shuttles heading off world."

"Were you able to ascertain which direction they took? Did they enter hyperspace or come back down in another area of the planet?"

"From the direction they were heading, it appears the reports from the Ministry could be correct. They seemed to be heading for the Kamino station before they dropped of the sensors, sir."

"Is there a possibility that they jumped to hyperspace?"

"Doubtful sir, not that close to the planet and we're not sure their shuttles had FTL capability anyway sir."

"Okay, I want a starship anchored off the side of that station. I want it loaded with a contingent of Special Forces and I want the squadron of fighters ready to attack on my command. Let's see what we can do to rattle Raine," Aslam said. Now he had a clearer picture of where they had taken the President, he was ready to take action. This would not go unpunished.

Chapter 64

SecOps HQ

"What the hell is happening?" Chambers said when he saw the starship take up position off the starboard quarter of the station. They were using satellite feeds to give them a real-time picture of the station.

A squadron of Marauders left the starship to take up position nearby as well.

He knew what was happening a screen in front came alive with a face he instantly recognised.

"General Aslam, to what do we owe the pleasure?" he said trying to keep it civil.

"You can tell whoever you have on that station, or about to enter it, to back off right now. This situation is now under the jurisdiction of the CDF, we'll handle things from here," Aslam said getting straight to the point.

"Now just hold on a moment General, we don't yet have confirmation that President Harada is being held there. If you go crashing in there without proof you will be in violation of God knows how many laws. Let me remind you sir, that station is privately owned and therefore is private property."

"And let me remind you, Director, that the safety of the President is my main concern. We have enough evidence to go on to order the attack on that station, so if you don't want your people caught in the crossfire then I suggest you call them off, now."

Clearly the general wasn't backing down and wasn't about to be threatened off this either.

"When are you ordering the attack?" he asked.

"The fighters make their first run in five minutes. By then the troops will be ready to perform their ingress to the station. You have until then to inform your people what is about to happen, after that, it'll be too late."

C made a cutting gesture, a thumb across his throat and the vid-feed was severed.

"Get me Pryde right now," he said.

"I'm a bit busy right now sir," Duncan said when he heard the call come through.

"You have five minutes after that the fighters parked off your starboard bow will commence their first attack run on the station. That will be followed by a consignment of Special Forces making a run to release the President from Raine's clutches. Whatever you're thinking of doing, I suggest you do it fast," C said.

Chapter 65

"Five minutes? We haven't even gotten on board the station yet," Sanchez said after hearing the call. Duncan had included her in the comm link.

The two of them had gone across to the station from their ship and were standing on the hull next to a hatch.

"We'd better hurry then," Duncan said coldly.

Operating the hatch from outside, they went inside and waited for the airlock to allow them inside the rest of the station.

"What now? This has to change the plan," she said as the inner hatch opened.

"A little bit," Duncan agreed.

The corridor ahead of them was empty. Duncan had chosen this ingress point as it was deserted most of the time. The most traffic on the station was centred around the command-and-control deck.

There was a computer terminal on the wall opposite the hatch. Duncan accessed it using his PIN. He needed to see what was happening on this station, he had a feeling the communications centre was a cover for the real purpose of what this station was built for. He also thought it had to do with why he'd brought the President here and not anywhere else on the planet, or even off world.

Scrolling through multiple screens he searched for something, not entirely sure what exactly he was looking for but knowing he would understand the instant he saw it.

There it was, he had it.

Turning to look at Sanchez he said, "I know what he's planning, and it's worse than we ever thought."

"Sir, a CDF starship has parked off our starboard bow along with a squadron of Marauder fighters," ops warned.

"I told you they wouldn't just stand by and do nothing," Harada said.

Raine turned to Kaufman who had listened to the conversation between the two of them with disdain. He couldn't care less about Raine's motives in this he just wanted what was promised him, absolution from all his past deeds and money, lots of money.

"Things are escalating Raine, I hope you have a plan for this," he said.

Raine snapped him a glance as sharp as a dagger, "Of course I have, nothing here is by chance, I have planned for every eventuality."

To ops he said, "Activate shields and charge the weapons. Bring the close quarter guns online and power up the rail guns."

"You intend to fight then?" Kaufman said with a smile.

"Did you expect anything else?" Raine asked.

"Shields at full power sir, close quarter defence guns targeting the fighters and the rail guns are all powered up," came the reply.

"Target the Coalition Headquarters with the rail guns," Raine said.

Kaufman smiled broadly, "You're using kinetic bombardment, cool," he said.

"Open fire," Raine said and the weapons controller fired the rail guns at the planet below.

"Was that what I think it was?" Sanchez asked as they heard the rail guns fire.

"They just fired rail guns," Duncan replied hardly believing what he was hearing.

"Who are they firing at, the CDF starship?" Sanchez asked.

"It didn't sound like that to me. It sounded like they fired toward Terra II."

"Holy shit!" she replied when the enormity of that hit her.

"Come on we have to find Harada fast. This is only going to get worse. Now they drew first blood, the CDF will retaliate and the gloves will come off."

He saw Sanchez's expression harden as she knew what they had to do now.

No holds barred.

The Coalition Headquarters received a direct hit from the first salvo from the rail gun.

The tungsten rod struck the roof of the building with enough force to batter right through into the ground smashing through everything in its path right through to the foundation of the building and beyond.

The resulting explosion was equivalent to dropping a small nuke on the building. A shockwave spread out destroying all in its path flattening buildings for a distance of almost three miles in every direction. Dirt and rubble were thrown up into the air to cover an even greater distance as it mushroomed out into the atmosphere.

No one could survive the attack and the actual death toll would only be finally recorded days after the attack when all the rubble was cleared and fully investigated. At the moment though Terra II's ability to co-ordinate a retaliatory strike was hampered by the headquarters of the CDF having been flattened.

Other areas of the city were flattened in the same way as they too were targeted by the rail guns. In moments huge sections of the city were completely destroyed.

In one swift move, Raine had slaughtered hundreds of thousands of innocent people.

Chapter 66

SecOps HQ

Everyone in the Situation Room stood aghast at what was displayed on the main monitor. They had been watching things unfold using satellite feeds and when the station opened fire with the rail guns they saw, in vivid detail the effects.

Hands were covering mouths as tears ran down faces and above all, there was a funeral silence covering the room.

Chambers was the first to break this silence. "Get me the captain of that CDF starship, now," he barked, even his voice was beginning to break with the emotions he was fighting to keep under control.

The link was enabled and C said, "This is Director Chambers of the Ministry, I am taking command of this operation. You need to open fire on that station, before it can fire again. Do you understand Captain?"

There was a pause and finally a voice replied, "But sir, the President is still on board."

"I understand Captain and if they fire again how many more thousands of lives will be lost? Open fire now, I take full responsibility. You need to disable that station now."

"Copy that sir," the captain replied.

"Now get me Pryde and fast," C said.

"Let me guess sir, you just ordered the starship to open fire on us," Duncan said when C called him. He'd tied Sanchez into the call as usual, it was important she know what was going on as much as he did.

"I had no choice. They will fire on the station, with everything they have, fighters, the full arsenal will be brought to bear so you have little time left. Duncan, do you think Raine still has some of the Omega Five virus on board?"

"It's doubtful sir, or he would've used it by now, at the very least he would have threatened us with it. He probably used it all against the refugee campsites. There are no guarantees he isn't making more of it somewhere though."

"Your priorities are clear here then. The President's safety and learning if Raine has any more of the virus, everything else is secondary, and Duncan, hurry. You have even less time now that they drew first blood, the gloves have just come off."

"Copy that sir," Duncan said then closed the call.

As he looked at his partner, he saw the fear and determination in her eyes.

"Let's get this done," she said.

Harada was silent after watching the attack on the surface of the planet, the same as everyone else on the Command-and-Control deck of the station.

Even Kaufman was quiet as he watched the destruction unfold below. Only Raine seemed to be undisturbed by what had happened. He turned to the other two men with a huge grin on his face.

"See how it feels Harada, to have control stripped away from you. To have to watch your own people die in front of your eyes unable to do anything to prevent it," he said enjoying the pain etched across the president's face.

"I have to give you credit Marcus, I knew you were an angry sonofabitch but I never realised how much of a mad crazy fool you were as well," Kaufman said his eyes wide with shock. The enormity of what had just happened was hitting home and he realised he was forever ties to the man who murdered millions of civilians just to get back at one man. He was truly insane and as he looked at him, he wondered how he had missed it from the very start.

Raine glanced around the room seeing the shocked, wide-eyed expressions of everyone present and grew angry.

"What? You all knew what was going to happen here, you all signed on for this so don't even pretend to be shocked," he shouted at them.

"Sir, we have incoming missiles from the starship," ops said as his attention was drawn to the screens by the warning alarms.

"Bring the rail guns to bear and order the fighters to engage the enemy," he replied, his military training taking over.

The station was rocked by several explosions from the missiles that struck the shields, weakening them significantly.

Lights flickered as systems were overloaded trying to compensate for the strikes they were taking.

Sparks flew from consoles and small fires burst out across the deck. Fire retardant foam was sprayed over them containing them before they could build to anything dangerous.

Raine sat in the command chair his eyes darting from one screen to another as he assessed the attack trying to see if there was a pattern to their strategy or if it was merely an all-out attack hoping to overwhelm them.

He saw the fighters flying around the starship that had also released its own fleet of one-man fighter craft. Dog fights were breaking out all around the ship as some attacked and others defended.

Meanwhile the starship continued to fire on them.

"Hit them with the rail guns," he said knowing that several hits at this range would devastate the ship and end this fight fast.

"Rail guns coming on target sir," ops replied.

"As soon as you get a target lock open fire," Raine said.

Chapter 67

On the bridge of the starship, Captain Robinson was in control. A veteran of many battles in space he had long hoped to never have to engage another ship in space. Yet here he was. That considered, he was determined to put all of his experience to ensuring his ship came out of this battle safe and sound and above all, victorious.

"Sir, they are bringing their rail guns to bear on us," ops warned.

"Bring our own plasma rail guns to bear on them, target their guns and open fire," Robinson said quickly yet calmly.

"Helm take evasive action, move us away from their rail guns, give our guys time to target them," he said.

The large starship moved to port and up away from the movement of the station's rail guns giving their gunners time to ensure they had their target within their sights.

The plasma rail guns opened fire sending out slugs of plasma energy at the opposite rail guns on the station. The plasma slug impacted the weapons blowing them apart along with a good portion of the station. The defence shields did little to prevent the slugs passing through unable to deflect or absorb the massive amounts of energy being thrust at them.

With a huge hole in the station now preventing the shields to function fully, they collapsed, leaving the station undefended.

The fleet of fighter craft continued to engage the defenders and explosions lit up the dark space for a brief instant as ships exploded only for the flames to flicker out to nothing as the vacuum of space smothered them.

The damage done to the station began to exact a toll and more systems began to fail as further explosions ran through the interior.

"Target that station with missiles, give them everything we have," Robinson ordered.

Duncan and Sanchez were almost knocked off their feet as the rail guns were destroyed in a huge explosion that rocked the entire structure.

"What the fuck was that?" Sanchez asked as she got back to her feet.

"If I didn't know better, I would have to say they just took out the rail guns," Duncan replied.

Other explosions began to rock the station then, giving them cause for concern.

"How are we supposed to do our job with what little time we have left?" she asked looking around. They were near a porthole that gave them a view of the outside. They could see, quite clearly, the battle being waged in between the station and the starship by the two squadrons of fighters. The fighters that were being destroyed looked for an instant like stars winking in then out as debris was flung outward from the silent blasts.

"Come on, we have to find the president before this place is blown apart," Duncan said.

"Are you just going to stay here and watch as this place gets destroyed?" Kaufman shouted above the din of consoles blowing up.

"Leave if you want to, I'm staying here," Raine snarled at him like a feral creature cornered by a pack of dogs.

"I didn't come here to die, this is madness," Kaufman reiterated.

"Go then, what's stopping you?" Raine said.

"I'm taking him with me, I can use him as leverage," he said pointing at the president.

Raine grabbed Harada by the arm, "He's staying here with me," he said.

"Have it your way, I'm taking my men and getting off this thing before they blow it out of the sky," he said and left the bridge in a hurry.

Harada looked from Kaufman to Raine and knew his last hope of getting off this station had just walked off.

Raine saw the fear in his eyes, "Good, you're finally getting it. You are going to die here, with me but not before I take everything from you," he said.

Chapter 68

Duncan and Sanchez were getting near to the Command-and-Control deck when they saw Kaufman exiting through a door.

He wasn't alone though, there were three of his men with him. It was the team that had delivered Harada to Raine.

Duncan and his partner had their SAP10s in their hands firing at the three men. Sanchez was the first to fire, dropping two of them before Duncan had time to even react leaving the last one for him. Three bullets, one for each which left Kaufman on his own.

They locked eyes and the large militia leader ran at him full tilt firing his own pistol as he ran. The first bullet zipped past Duncan's head, the air sizzling near his ear. The second passed under his arm almost puncturing the fabric of his EVA suit. The third bullet struck the gun in his hand sending his SAP 10 spinning across the floor.

The shock of having his gun ripped from his hand sent a flash of pain ripping through his fingers. Shaking his hand to relieve the numbness he was hit around the waist as Kaufman tackled him.

The two of them went crashing to the ground watched by Sanchez who covered the bodies with her SAP 10.

Duncan squirmed free before Kaufman could start any ground and pound tactics. He pushed himself clear then scrambled to his feet as fast as he could.

Kaufman lashed out with a leg hoping to sweep him sending him back to the ground, but Duncan saw it coming and jumped over the leg.

As the other man got to his feet as well, they faced each other. Duncan had lost his pistol before the tackle so it was down to close quarter combat now.

The large man aimed a few blows at him testing his reflexes and Duncan blocked each or dodged back out of range.

Kaufman threw a straight right aiming at Duncan's face which he slipped allowing it to pass over his left shoulder as he dipped. Coming back up he rammed his left fist into the ribs of his attacker then followed up with a right hook to the face. Kaufman bellowed his rage and threw a flurry of punches at Duncan, a combination trying to get through his guard.

Duncan blocked or deflected each blow as he was pushed back on the defensive more with each blow.

He felt the wall against his back and knew there was nowhere else to go, he was trapped.

"Let me take the shot," screamed Sanchez at him as she tried to get a clean shot off.

"I've got this," Duncan said calmly.

"You got nothing," snarled Kaufman.

Duncan saw his opportunity and struck. A straight fingered jab landed on Kaufman's unprotected throat knocking his head back. His eyes went wide from the shock as his throat constricted immediately.

Duncan pushed his away as he snapped his blade free from the sheath on his thigh. As Kaufman tried to recover, he reached for Duncan who blocked the leading arm then slashed the bicep. Moving fast he slashed one of his attacker's thighs severing an artery. Blood quickly ran from the wound and he tried to clamp his hand over it to stop it.

Duncan stabbed that arm ripping the blade free to open up a massive wound in that also.

He saw fear in his eyes as he knew he was about to die. Dropping to his knees, already weakened from blood loss, Duncan stepped forward clamping a hand on the back of Kaufman's head then rammed the blade into the side of his neck. Blood ran down the front of the big man's shirt as his artery was cut. Pulling the blade out and across Duncan opened up the throat allowing the blood to run more freely. He saw the light go out of his eyes as he died with a gurgle slipping out of the gash in his neck. With a squelching sound the dead man fell over.

"That was intense," Sanchez observed with a sigh of relief.

Wiping the blade free of blood on Kaufman's chest Duncan said, "Let's get in there."

With his hand on the door release he was about to open it when another massive explosion rocked the station.

"I think we just ran out of time," Sanchez said.

Chapter 69

Raine saw the door open once more and he thought Kaufman had had second thoughts and was returning. His mouth dropped open when he saw who it was though.

He was just recovering from the last blast that had shaken the station thinking it would soon be over when the newcomers arrived, no doubt to spoil his fun.

"Give it up Raine, it's over. There's nowhere to run this time," Duncan shouted, aiming his gun at him.

"He's not going anywhere, he wants to die here and watch Terra II burn," Harada screamed at them.

"How very 'Nero' of you Marcus, but what's the point of that?" Duncan said.

"I want Harada to witness what was coming to Altair, the destruction his policies would bring to my world over time. The slow agonizing death to all who lived there. Forgotten by the bureaucrats who make the decisions because it doesn't affect them. Only this time, I've brought all that here, to his world and he's witnessing it all in minutes instead of years," Raine answered unapologetically.

"There has to be another way surely," Sanchez pleaded.

"There is no other way. This is the only way to make them realise they cannot play games with people's lives. This is not a game of chess; we are not simply pieces to be moved around a board with no consequence to the player. This is real life and I want him to experience it all."

"Have you brought your case before the Coalition Council to see if there was another way?" Duncan asked.

"Of course, I did. I begged for them to reconsider but they ignored my pleas and said there was nothing they could do; the decision had been made."

Duncan looked at the frightened face of the president. "Who was making money out of this Mister President?" he asked, the last two words laden heavily with contempt. He had an idea why the council had summarily thrown out Raine's request and was about to force the answer from the one person who knew what it was.

Harada's eyes went wide in mock innocence. "I have no idea what you're talking about," he said.

"You see, when anyone replies like that, they are always hiding something," Duncan said recognising the avoidance technique.

Harada looked around the room for support, when he saw he was getting none he finally said, "Aren't you two supposed to be rescuing me?"

"As soon as you answer my question, sir. Who benefitted from having the refugees placed on Altair? You either tell me now or we leave," Duncan said.

"You can't leave me here, you can't do that," Harada screamed at him.

"Watch me," Duncan said his expression as cold and hard as stone.

"No one will know, I'll just report that we arrived too late to save you. The station was destroyed with everyone on board," he added to force his point home and show Harada the reality of his situation. He was not in control here, and never had been.

Finally, Harada saw he had no way out of this so he said, "Okay, there was a group of us who saw an opportunity to push home a new deal on terraforming. New safety protocols were needed obviously, and new plants had to be made to implement them properly."

"And this group were the ones who made these new plants I take it," Duncan said.

Harada looked at him and simply nodded.

"What about the refugees?" Sanchez asked.

"Something had to be done about them, we had to put them somewhere and fast so we chose Altair, it was the nearest planet and it was more efficient to place them there than transport them across the galaxy," Harada replied.

"By most efficient you mean the cheapest option. It would cost less to dump them there than transport them to a planet that could accommodate them, that's what you're really saying, isn't it?" Duncan said.

Again, Harada simply nodded.

"So, I was right all along, this has been all about making money after all," Raine said. He had been listening to the president recounting the reason that was behind all of this and his anger grew with every word he heard. Finally, he could contain it no longer.

He reached for a pistol, brought it up to Harada's face and shot him point blank. The move was so fast and unexpected it caught everyone else off guard, all except Duncan.

He saw the move and could have stopped it from happening. He watched, not in apathy this time but with empathy.

He could see all the pain Raine was feeling, all the anger and frustration that had built up to this one moment.

Did he condone all of his actions leading to this point, no, obviously not but he allowed him this one last act of revenge against the man who had caused all his pain and suffering, before he shot him too.

In the blink of an eye, it was over. Two more dead bodies lay on the floor and the threat was done with.

Sanchez stared at the two bodies in a state of shock which was destroyed when another explosion rocked the station once more.

Looking around at all the systems that were going offline, sparks flying everywhere and smaller blasts erupting across the work stations brought her out of her reverie.

"We need to leave, now," Duncan said.

"You'll get no argument from me on that score," she replied and the two of them made for the door.

Chapter 70

As the satellite's destruction increased, Duncan and Sanchez raced from the Command-and-Control deck as fast as they could. It had already been vacated by the crew as soon as the shields went down and the plasma rail guns broke through followed by the missiles. A few had remained to man certain operations either out of loyalty or because they had the same insane sense of purpose as Raine once had. With him dead though, they had no reason to remain, so they too fled the dying station.

They knew it was over and so they ran for the escape pods as soon as they could. None of them had the same commitment as Raine nor his insane determination to see this through to the bitter end, except for those last few.

The floor beneath their feet shook almost as if it was trying to throw them off. They came to a junction in the corridor and saw the way ahead blocked by a fallen bulkhead. Wiring showed clear in a tangled mess hanging in ribbons from the hole in the wall. Sparks danced across from shattered circuitry as electricity danced and arced between junction points.

"Dead end," Sanchez said, stating the obvious.

"There has to be another way out of here," Duncan said ignoring her comment.

Turning back, they ran back they way they had come. There was an elevator at the end.

"We need a stairwell, we can't trust the elevators will still work not with all the explosions around this place," Duncan said.

"We're running out of time here, this place is falling apart around us," Sanchez said, her voice shaking as she felt panic build.

Duncan prised open a door that led to a turbo shaft. He peered inside and saw there was a ladder attached to the side of the vertical shaft.

"This is our best bet of getting out of here," he said to her. "Follow me," he added. He climbed inside and started down the ladder. Sanchez quickly followed him inside the shaft and they both scrambled down.

Hand over hand they moved down the ladder going as fast as they could. As fast as they went, they were careful not to take a miss step as they knew if that happened, they would fall to their doom inside this shaft.

They saw an exit hatch on the next level down which exited into another corridor.

Debris from above began falling forcing the two of them to press their bodies against the ladder to avoid being knocked off.

"Hurry," Duncan urged as he began to climb down again once the debris had finished raining down on them. Reaching the hatch, he forced it open and climbed through. He waited for Sanchez and made sure she left the turbo shaft safely.

Duncan looked around for an avenue of escape. A crack appeared in the wall by their side a few paces in front of them. They saw it begin to widen and move across the wall, down onto the deck and stretch out in front of them.

"Shit!" Duncan said, "we need to go in that direction," he added dragging her after him as he chased after the crack.

As they ran, they caught up with the crack which was widening slowly, the further it travelled through the station. They saw it between their steps and it became a literal race for survival.

Other figures emerged from rooms on this deck, Duncan caught a sight of their panic-stricken faces. Wide eyed stares with teeth bared in a rictus of anger, fear and desperation etched across their faces.

Duncan barrelled his way through some of them heading toward a hatch or escape pod of some kind.

Bodies fell or were pushed out of the way with no regard for their safety. Duncan's only concern now was to get himself and his partner off the quickly disintegrating station.

Angry faces greeted him as they barged through them. Hands grabbed for them and it became more difficult to move through the throng.

A fist landed on Duncan's jaw as the crowd reacted to the two intruders wearing EVA suits in their midst.

Sanchez was grabbed from behind, hands clamping on her arms holding her back. A fist thumped into her gut doubling her over. Unable to defend herself due to the hands holding her arms against her sides.

Two men grabbed Duncan, one around the neck, the other around his chest. He lashed out with his right leg kicking the man advancing on him from the front. His kick propelled his attacker staggering backwards to collide with the men holding Sanchez.

Duncan then jerked his head back into the face of the man holding him around the neck. The grip around his neck was released a little and he was able to move a little more freely. Twisting and turning he was able to free his arms more enabling him to free one of them enough to slam an elbow back into the ribs of the man holding him.

Pulling the other one over his shoulder he threw him onto the deck.

This fight had not gone as well as expected and the group backed off becoming more wary of this duo.

Sanchez had freed herself with a blow to the man holding her arms once he had released them after the collision from behind.

Duncan grabbed her once more by the arm.

"Let's go," he said dragging her out of harm's way.

"I don't need you to rescue me," she replied angrily.

"Really, you want to do this now?" he said.

He continued to run away from the group pulling her with him.

"Point taken," she said.

Some of them were members of Kaufman's militia and had weapons drawn. Shots followed the two agents down the corridor punching holes in the walls as they missed their targets.

Bullets hit the bulkhead close by Duncan's head and he ducked into a room. Sanchez hit the floor as bullets pounded the deck near her.

Reaching out, Duncan offered her a hand to pull her to safety.

"Take my hand, unless you can do it on your own?" he said.

Her lips pressed together she decided not to comment and took his hand instead.

He pulled her inside the room as she fired her pistol at the men chasing them. She dropped one which discouraged the others a little and they held back as they rethought their tactics.

Looking around Duncan realised they couldn't remain in here for too long.

"What now?" his partner asked.

"I'm working on it," he replied.

"Work faster," she urged.

"If you have a plan of your own, now's the time to say so."

She gave no comment just snapped him a sharp look.

He moved to the back of the room and saw a door around a corner.

"This way," he beckoned.

They were about to enter through the door when the other door crashed open. The armed militia burst through firing as they came. Bullets bounced off the wall of the corner just as the two agents disappeared through the other one.

Chapter 71

Mi7 Hq

The Situation Room was silent as all eyes were glued to the main monitor. The display screen showed the view from the Starship attacking the station.

The fighter craft zipped in and out of view as they fought an aerial battle for survival. Explosions briefly lit up the dark of space only to wink out just as suddenly.

The station was being chipped away and would soon succumb to its own destruction and the worried faces watched knowing that they had someone on board they knew and cared about.

One thing was certain, no more lives would be lost on the planet below as this attack had prompted the station to defend itself.

There was a huge gaping hole in the hull of the station where the rail guns used to be. This hole was widening as the integrity of the hull was compromised further with each new blow dealt to it. Explosions inside the station added to the mess destroying more of it from the inside out and anyone attempting to flee now had precious little time left.

"Get moving you two," C said quietly as he watched, his hands firmly clasped together in anguish.

Once they were through the door, Duncan and Sanchez noticed they were trapped.

There was only one door to this room and they had just gone through it.

"Up there," Duncan said indicating a panel in the ceiling that had a gap in it. It was a false ceiling and if his theory was correct, there would be a crawl way above their heads. It wasn't ideal, but it was their only choice.

Jumping up on a table he quickly moved the panel free, pushing it up into the gap in the ceiling so he could see inside.

Grabbing the edges of the opening he jumped up off the table and using the power of his arms alone, lifted himself up into the crawl space. He was used to this kind of thing, being an experienced climber, this was nothing new to him.

Within seconds he had squirmed inside the small crawl space and was looking down into the room.

"Grab my hands and I'll pull you up," he said, "Hurry before they come through that door.

Reaching down Duncan grabbed hold of her hands and lying on his stomach, he pulled her up until she could grab the edge of the opening.

"Right, now pull yourself up," he said reaching over her to grab her waist and pull her up that way. It was a struggle for her but she was determined to get inside the crawl space. Once her stomach was on the edge all she had to do was throw up a knee and then she had a better position and could get more leverage to get inside with her partner.

"Where to now?" she asked breathing hard from her exertions.

"Follow me," he said and he began crawling down the narrow tunnel.

Before long the damage done to the station took its toll and the inside of the crawl space collapsed beneath them dropping them into another room. As they landed in a tumble the rest of the station seemed to fall with them.

The floor tilted steeply and them with it. Arms and legs flailed as they scrambled for a hold on anything as they slid to a gaping hole in the hull.

Seeing what was through the hole they snapped the helmets back on their heads.

They slid through the hole into space. Their momentum added by the escaping atmosphere sucked the two of them out into space away from the station.

Duncan fired his thruster pack and so did Sanchez. Powered by the packs they moved away from the station as fast as they could.

"Ship, we need an exfil immediately," Duncan said in his comm link.

"On my way Commander," the AI replied.

In just a few moments the ship appeared in front of them and they pulled up before they ran into it.

Entering through the hatch they were soon powering through space away from the station.

More explosions ripped through what was left of the station building up to one last massive detonation that blasted what was left of it spreading debris over miles of space.

Duncan and Sanchez arrived on the bridge in time to witness the final destruction of the station. The fighter fleet pulled away from the fight after the explosion leaving the others to return to the CDF starship that had been attacking the station.

As the two agents watched all this Sanchez said, "Well, thank God that's finally over."

Duncan sat in his chair and nodded.

"Finally," he agreed.

Chapter 72

Mi7, Hq

"So, what happens now?" Sanchez asked.

They had landed at the HQ and gone straight to C's office to report in.

Both of them were weary and ached from head to toe but grateful that they had come out of it alive.

They dropped into the chairs in front of the desk with C facing them.

"First off I must congratulate you both for a job well done. To answer your question though, there is a lot of work to be done. There will have to be a new President sworn in and then the rebuilding will start. Several areas of this planet have been decimated. It's a good job the slugs fired from that station were not nuclear or larger or we could've been facing an extinction level event," C replied sombrely.

Duncan was quiet through C's explanation. He said, "We had a lucky escape today."

"Yes, we did," C said, "now you two need to go grab some rest. The full debrief can continue tomorrow when hopefully we will know a little more about this whole situation."

"I'm okay sir, we can do this now if you want," Duncan said.

"No Agent Pryde, you've been on the go for the last day or so, you too Sanchez. You need to rest. I want you both fully awake before we go into the debrief. Like I said, we should know a little more by then."

Duncan didn't want to leave, he felt there was still so much to do, to learn. He felt there was something they had all missed but he couldn't quite put his finger on it. Perhaps C was right, maybe a good night's sleep would help to refocus his mind fully.

Getting to his feet he said, "Thank you sir. I'll report back in the morning."

Sanchez was on her feet following him out of the door. "Thank you, sir," she said at the door.

Duncan went back home to his apartment. As he drove through the streets, he witnessed signs of the recent attack in the shocked faces of everyone he saw. In today's climate social media was everywhere and the attack had been shown live on every news media outlet throughout the Interweb.

New London had been hit but where the HQ was, near the river had been away from any activity. Instead, the centre of the city where the Coalition Council headquarters were located had taken a direct hit and the area around it for at least five miles had been completely destroyed.

Clouds of dust filled the air from the blast and people were walking around in a daze lucky to be alive.

He saw in many of their eyes the question of how had they been spared and why. It wasn't a question he had an answer to so he diverted his eyes and headed for home.

Once he was inside his apartment, he realised just how fatigued he was. His entire body ached from the blows he had taken. His muscles ached so much from his exertions that at times it hurt to even lift an arm or take a stumbling step. He went straight to his bedroom and dropped face first down onto his bed and in a few seconds was fast asleep.

Duncan woke feeling refreshed so he stripped off and took a shower. As the hot water hit his flesh, all the aches and pains from the previous day seemed to melt away.

After a thorough cleansing he dried himself off and put on some clean clothes. He liked the feel of a freshly cleaned shirt as it caressed his skin almost as much as slipping between clean sheets on a bed.

As he went into his kitchen to get some breakfast, his hair still slightly damp from his shower he heard a familiar chime in his ear from a call coming through.

Recognising the caller he said, "Good morning Stef, I was just about to get some breakfast then come in."

"Make it fast then Duncan, there's been a development and we're recalling all personnel to base," replied Goodchild sounding worried.

"I'm on my way," he said and ended the call.

Something had happened and it must be bad for C to recall all personnel. Whatever it was he would soon find out. Grabbing a supplement bar, he picked up his holster with his SAP 10 and placed it around his back and shoulders before shrugging into a light jacket. He was out the door in moments heading to his car.

Chapter 73

Temporary Council HQ

Vice President Calvin Parris took the chair at the head of the long oak table. At fifty-eight he thought his present run, in politics was coming to an end. The Vice President's position was the highest he had achieved in his long career and how things had stood he didn't think he would have had another run at the top position, until yesterday.

His deep brown skin glistened under the lights in the hastily prepared room, it was a conference room in the largest hotel in New London, procured for this meeting and until further notice while a new, more permanent headquarters could be made available.

The news of the attack had hit them all hard and he was still reeling from the repercussions of it all. Protocol demands that should the President be incapacitated in any way then the VP stands in as a replacement.

Parris had always wanted to be President, but not like this. He wanted to be the elected official not the substitute. That was not the case here though, so he couldn't think like that. He was placed in office not through any act of congress by the electorate but out of necessity and he would fill that necessity to the best of his ability.

He took a deep breath as he was about to start the meeting.

———

Outside the hotel a jet copter came in to hover above it. Long ropes were tossed out of both sides of the long passenger section on which soldiers in battle gear rappelled to the ground.

As the first soldiers hit the ground, they had their rifles out guarding the entrance supplying cover to those who followed. The last to land out of the ten-man group was dressed in the same gear but had shoulder flashes of a Colonel.

He issued order through hand signals and the group made their way into the hotel.

The guards on duty in the lobby conceded control to this superior officer unaware of his true intentions, thinking they were merely being replaced.

Unobstructed, the small group made their way to the Conference Hall, where the meeting was about to take place.

———

"What new steps are being taken to prevent what happened yesterday, ever happening again?" he asked.

"Sir every government department has someone ready to step into the top position. The CDF has a new commander, General Borelli and he is taking charge of all troop movements and for the time being, your personal security detail until the Presidential Security Service has appointed a new detail," replied Chief of Staff Walter Coggins.

Parris took what was being said then began speaking.

"The first order of business is getting the emergency services up to speed at the impact sites. I want security added to these areas, we can't have looters coming in scavenging. As soon as these sites have been cleared and the bodies counted, I want them identified so their families can be informed. Once that has been completed, we can start to rebuild. In the meantime, these areas will have to be cordoned off and travel routes put in place to circumnavigate around them."

"We are on that sir," Coggins assured him.

"Are we absolutely sure that the danger is over?" he asked.

"As far as we know sir, yes. The Ministry has informed us that the culprit has been dealt with and is no longer a threat."

"That's something I suppose," Parris said looking down at his hands. "Is there anything else before we close this meeting?" he asked.

Before anyone could reply, the door burst open and a group of armed men burst in,

"Sorry I'm late gentlemen, I promise to make up for it though now we are here," the man in front said.

"What's the meaning of this, and who the hell are you?" Parris asked sternly jumping to his feet.

"I'm Colonel Anton Hausner, and I am your new Commander in Chief," said the tall man.

Chapter 74

Mi7 Hq

Duncan arrived at headquarters and went straight to the office where he was greeted by Stephanie Goodchild. Her normal sunny expression nowhere to be seen, instead, she wore a troubled frown which did not bode well for the coming day.

"I got here as soon as I could," he said.

"He's in his office, you'd better go right in," she replied forsaking their usual flirty banter.

Sensing this was as urgent as he'd suspected he went right in.

Sitting behind his desk, his usual stoic expression had taken the day off and a new, darker one had taken root.

"Morning sir," he said on entry. He strode up to the desk and stood with a straight back, hands clasped behind his back.

"Sit down Pryde, I've received some troubling news this morning which, after yesterday's events, could be rather difficult to deal with," C said.

Sitting down Duncan waited for his boss to elaborate further.

"It seems that a certain Colonel Hausner and a cadre of his most loyal men have gone AWOL from their posts. As soon as they were reported missing a search of their trackers was initiated and they were found here in New London."

"Where abouts sir?" Duncan asked.

"At the hotel that had been commissioned for the new Council meeting taking place today," C told him.

Duncan sensed there was more to this so he waited for more details to come.

"A check into the Colonel was completed as soon as he and his men went missing and it seems he has been rather vocal of late about current policy regarding the CDF. His opinion is on record stating he thought the CDF was growing weaker and not dealing appropriately with threats on the Coalition."

"If that's the case then sir then this would be an ideal time for him to let those in power know he'd been right all along," Duncan said, suspecting there might be a little more to this than a simple 'I told you so'.

"I agree, and it seems we were right to believe that. All communication with the meeting has been terminated, the building has been cut off completely. It seems that Colonel Hausner might be attempting a coup."

"How did he gain access to the meeting sir?"

"You know what soldiers are like, respecting the chain of command. All it would require was for him to turn up and inform the guards they were either relieved or he'd been summoned to the meeting. I doubt any lower rank would question an order given by a colonel, especially not in these times when everyone is scrambling to look for someone to step up and take command. The average soldier works on the principle that someone higher up the chain knows what they're doing and their job is simply to follow orders."

"I understand that sir, and I take your point about everyone looking for someone to step up and take command. What I don't get is what does he hope to gain? Does he think he can take over the entire CDF with a handful of men loyal to him, what about the other officers and troops who are loyal to their commanders?"

"As you know, General Aslam was killed in the attack with most of the president's general staff so until the next in line can be appointed as head of the CDF it seems Hausner is taking matters into his own hands. At the moment, if he has control of the VP and can get him on his side then he will have a power base that would be unassailable. At this point in time I doubt that has happened. I think that could be his objective though so we must act fast to ensure everyone in that room is safe and Hausner doesn't have time to complete whatever it is he has in mind."

"Agreed sir."

"Agent Sanchez is already prepped and ready to go, I want you to join her and get there to assess the situation."

"I'm on it, sir," he said getting to his feet.

"Once you have a clear picture of what's going on in there, I want you to make sure our fears do not materialise. Take extreme measures if you have to but a coup is not happening today, not on my watch, especially not after losing the President, is that understood?"

"Perfectly clear sir."

"Good luck, Sanchez is waiting for you on your ship."

Duncan left the office and made his way to the landing pad where Sanchez was waiting for him. He didn't stop to speak to Goodchild as he was closing off his emotions as he had a job to do. It seemed that this mission was still on and now he was dealing with the repercussions of events started by the actions of Raine.

This was something that could have consequences for the entire Coalition, he had to shut this thing down and fast.

Chapter 75

Council Meeting

"What do you want here?" Parris asked. He was clearly disturbed by the intrusion of so many armed men who all gave off the most hostile vibes. The tension in the room had escalated the moment they had entered.

"It's quite simple, I want to restore balance and stability to the Coalition. Isn't that what we all want?" Hausner replied.

"I get the impression though you are willing to use force to achieve that goal. That isn't democracy that's you becoming a tyrant, a despot. The Coalition will never stand for such a thing," Parris stated.

"They will never know."

"Oh, you think your appearance here has gone unnoticed, or your disappearance from your post won't be noted on a record somewhere? If you think that Colonel, then you are deluded and I doubt you are anything like that at all."

"Granted, those things will be on record but they can be explained away when you inform the Council that you summoned me here to act as your new head of the CDF."

"I can't do that."

"Can't, or won't?" Hausner asked taking a step forward hoping to intimidate.

"Either, the result is the same," Parris told him standing his ground.

Hausner stared into his eyes trying to gauge the type of man he was. This was not the same man as Harada had been, here was a man with principles, he had backbone, but he also had compassion too.

Taking out his sidearm Hausner shot the man standing next to Parris. The shot echoed around the room and Parris moved involuntarily to the side away from the sound that almost burst his eardrum.

Blood splattered the side of his face as the man's head was burst open from the high velocity shell piercing his skull before he dropped to the floor. He was mercifully dead before he hit the floor.

Parris rose to his full height once more and glared at the colonel in front of him. His eyes seemed to spark with repressed rage as his gaze bored into his soul.

"Are you sure I can't persuade you?" Hausner asked. His tone hinted that he was unbalanced so he had to proceed with caution here or more lives would be lost.

"He was a good man, he didn't deserve to die pointlessly like that, he didn't deserve to die at all, but definitely not to make a point like that," Parris said keeping his voice as calm and measured as he possibly could. He knew any sign of hostility toward these men would only result in more deaths.

"Did it make the point though?" Hausner asked calmly as he took his eyes from Parris to survey the room. He saw a sea of frightened faces as he picked his next target.

"The point that you will do anything to get what you want? That you are determined to get your own way? That you are not quite sane? Yes, that point was hammered home quite succinctly."

"Do you think it wise to antagonise me at this point? You've already cost one person their life, do you want to be the cause of another?"

"Let's get one thing clear here, Colonel. I am not responsible for the death of that man, you are. You pulled the trigger, not me. You clearly came in here to make a point and you were probably going to kill someone anyway to prove the validity of your cause. You made that decision before stepping through that door, that was you, not me. What happens next is down to you as well. You have a choice, you can walk away and return to duty or continue with this insane quest of yours but whatever the outcome, whatever happens, whoever dies next will be on your head, not mine," Parris said.

Hausner smiled in genuine respect for the man's courage, he felt it was a shame that he might have to kill this guy as he could have been an excellent president.

"Are you prepared to die sir, to back up that claim?" he asked.

"It comes with the job, so yes. As a matter of fact, we all are."

"Speak for yourself, I'm not prepared to die for this. This is just a job, a really good one, but a job just the same," a voice shouted from somewhere down the room.

Parris looked around to see who it was, recognising the voice and saw other faces mirroring his concern as well.

The room came alive with voices echoing the same comment.

"Me too."

"Nah ah, not me."

"I don't want to die either."

And it continued until almost all the room had joined in leaving Parris with a few people who, like him would stand strong against this threat.

"Wow," Hausner said looking around at all those people who had separated from the rest to stand as a group hoping they would survive this encounter.

Parris's eyes dropped for he had some idea what might happen next and didn't want to see it.

"You seem to be in the minority here," Hausner said then his gaze fell on the group and his mouth turned downwards in contempt.

"You lot think by turning against your boss here that you will survive this. Maybe take up a position on my new council," he said to which several of the group began to nod in agreement.

"What's to say though, that you wouldn't turn against me at the first sign of trouble. After all, you already did it once."

This brought a harsh reality home to them and they began looking around at each other, confusion turning to fear.

"I can't work with someone as disloyal as you lot," Hausner said and he gave a signal to his men who opened fire on them.

Bullets shredded their flesh making them dance like demented puppets as blood painted their clothes, their flesh as they were gunned down like rabid dogs.

When it was over Parris opened his eyes and looked up at the colonel.

"Tell me what you want from me," he said, all fight removed from him.

Chapter 76

The ship carrying Duncan and Sanchez came in to land on the landing pad close to the front of the hotel. It was reserved for shuttles arriving bringing guests so the landing had to be precise as it was larger than most shuttles that used this facility.

Sanchez looked across at her partner as she prepared to leave her seat and said, "Here we go again, once more into the breach dear friends."

Duncan looked at her, a slight head tilt as he was confused by her words.

"I'm paraphrasing Henry the Fifth by Shakespeare," she said, her eyes widening in surprise. "Are you not familiar with the classics?" she asked.

Duncan ignored the question, "We have work to do," he said instead. His mind was closed off to any stimuli that might give an emotional reaction now, totally under control, his one focus on the job at hand.

Wearing dark clothing, with fluid body armour underneath the two of them walked across from the ship towards the entrance of the hotel.

At the door they were greeted by an armed soldier who barred their path.

"I'm sorry sir, Ma'am, but access to the hotel is denied at this time," he said.

"It's okay soldier, we're expected," Duncan said as he tried to go past.

"No can-do sir, I can't let you pass, I have my orders," the soldier said and he looked away for just a second at Sanchez giving Duncan time to strike.

In a flash he had his SAP 10 out, the suppressor already fitted and up against the throat of the soldier. A slight pressure on the trigger sent a bullet through his throat almost severing his head. All anyone would have heard was a slight coughing sound as the bullet left the muzzle, having shot out the soldier's throat meant no sound would be issued from him.

Sanchez was getting used to his harsh tactics and didn't even flinch this time just walked past the dead body as she followed him through the lobby.

"Where is the Conference Room from here?" she asked as she caught up with him.

"It's on this floor at the back of the hotel," he said.

"I have a chopper waiting on the roof. We are leaving to a safe location where you will issue your orders to the entire Coalition, under my supervision, of course, and then we will start to make the galaxy a safer place to live," Hausner said as he ushered Parris toward the door.

Feeling helpless, Parris went along with it and they exited the room and went straight to the elevator.

The door at the back of the lobby suddenly opened and armed soldiers emerged followed by the colonel pushing Parris in front of him.

Duncan already had his SAP 10 ready and fired hitting the two soldiers leading the group, in the chest, knocking them back.

All the soldiers were wearing standard body armour but the new 10mil rounds passed through it like it wasn't there.

Two down and the others returned fire.

Bullets flew across the lobby and the two agents were caught out in the open. Eight soldiers firing at them meant they had to retreat and find some cover so they moved behind the reception desk.

The solid barrier surrounding the desk began to be chipped away by the barrage of ammo striking it. Splinters of wood flew into the air from every hit as they relentlessly chipped away at it.

Duncan thought he heard a voice shouting above the cacophony but he couldn't be sure until there was a cease fire.

The sudden silence was almost as deafening as the gunfire that preceded it.

"Where'd they go?" Sanchez asked as she peered around the edge toward where the shooters had been. Duncan too, stood up to take a look. He saw the door to the stairs next to the elevator.

"They've gone to the roof. They must have an exfil up there," he said.

Without a thought he was on his feet giving chase.

"Get to the roof and secure the chopper," Hausner said to his men, then singling out three of them said, "you remain here, give us covering fire, stop them from following us, understood?"

Nods from the soldiers in question was the answer he was looking for.

Pushing Parris up the stairs Hausner said, "Move Mister President, we have a flight to catch."

Chapter 77

"We have to stop them," Sanchez said as she ran toward the stairway door.

Duncan was a step behind her and as they reached the door he placed a restraining hand on her arm to stop her rushing through.

"They'll have planted someone there to catch us going through," he said when she glared at him angrily.

Opening the door a crack they were met by a hail of automatic gunfire that slammed into the other side of the door.

"Shit!" she said as they both moved back out of range.

Taking a grenade out of his weapons belt he primed it then tossed it through the crack in the door again.

The timer was set for three seconds so the soldiers left behind didn't have time to react or get clear before the explosion ripped through them.

The ensuing blast was felt on the other side of the door as the pressure wave tried to rip it clear. Holding on by one small hinge the door slammed back against the wall of the lobby then hung there like a one armed man hanging on for grim death.

Quickly Duncan ran through the gap left by the hanging door and ran up the stairs taking them three at a time. Keeping his breathing under control he powered up the stairs after Hausner and the rest of his team.

Sanchez was right behind him keeping pace, her pistol held out in front ready to fire.

The first two landing were covered with relative ease. No sign of who they were chasing so they increased their pace. Two more landings were navigated through and finally they caught sight of them.

A hailstorm of bullets stopped their advance as they hit the bend. Chips of wall peppered Duncan's hair as he came close to getting hit in the face by a well-aimed shot.

"Where are you taking him Colonel?" Duncan asked shouting above the noise of the gunfire.

"We have work to do to restore power to the Coalition," came the shouted reply.

"How, by killing innocent people?" Duncan asked.

"You wouldn't understand, what I'm about to do is beyond your tiny little mind's level of intelligence," Hausner shot back in a sneer.

"Wow, not only are you trying to kill me but you're insulting me as well," Duncan said in uncharacteristic sarcasm.

"You not only don't understand this but you can't stop it from happening either."

"I'll take that bet," Duncan replied.

He saw one of the soldiers show their head around the corner about to fire his rifle but Duncan shot first. His bullet took out the left eye of the soldier and the back of his head as it passed through his skull. As he tumbled down the stairs the other soldiers returned fire as they retreated up towards their destination.

The gunfire stopped and they heard a door open and slam shut after a brief pause. They had reached the roof.

"C'mon, we have to move," Duncan said as he took off after them.

His arms and legs pumped as he willed himself on to greater levels of exertion knowing he had to reach the roof to stop them leaving with the new President.

Reaching the top, he burst through the door to the roof without stopping to think. The chopper was there waiting and Hausner and his group were almost at the end of their journey. The soldiers turned to look his way and they opened fire.

Moving back around the side of the door frame they were under cover. Chips of concrete were sent spinning into the air from where the bullets slammed into the door frame.

"They're getting away," Sanchez said as she ducked her head down lower.

Taking another grenade from his pouch he primed it then tossed it over the heads of the soldiers. The small explosive device landed in front of two of the soldiers who were firing at them. The blast threw them into the air ripping them apart sending bloody body parts spinning across the rooftop.

Emerging from behind the block that held the door the two agents fired at the remaining soldiers careful not to hit the President.

As they took a step forward the sound of a fighter jet boomed across the sky deafening everyone. It came swooping in on an attack vector and opened up with its cannons.

"Get down," Duncan shouted as he dived onto his stomach. Sanchez followed suit and the two of them hit the ground as the cannon shells stitched a path through the soldiers.

Hausner had pushed Parris near the chopper out of harms way as the cannon fire tore up him and what was left of his men.

The fighter passed overhead having finished his attack run and Duncan was on his feet in a flash.

"Over here Mister President, run," he shouted and Parris complied running faster than he thought possible.

Duncan, Sanchez and Parris headed for the stairway door when Duncan spotted something that stopped them all.

"He's coming back," he said.

Sanchez pulled Parris through the door with her as Duncan watched what was going to happen. Standing in the doorway he watched as the fighter came in again this time firing a missile at the chopper.

"Oh shit!" Duncan said rushing through the door and slamming it after him.

"Run, get down those stairs, now," he screamed urging the other two into action.

They were one landing down when the missile struck. The explosion destroyed anything left on the roof. The blast blew the door into the stairwell with enough force to send it clattering after them. Fire followed it into the stairwell, flames lapping at their heels. The heat was so oppressive they could feel their skin begin to blister as they ducked down allowing the flames to pass over their heads.

It was over as fast as it had started and they were left on their knees huddled under their arms covering their heads, able to breathe once more.

"I think it's safe to say that the threat is over," Duncan said.

"Come on Mister President, let's get you to somewhere safe," Sanchez said.

The pilot of the jet took the aircraft out over the coat and said, "Target destroyed," into the encrypted comm link he was using which isolated himself from the channels used from the CDF Airbase where he had taken off from moments earlier.

This mission had been sanctioned at the last second when news of Hausner's assault on the Council meeting had reached his control. He didn't know who it was just that when he, she, or they gave an order he was obligated to carry that out, no matter the consequences. Such was the discipline within the organisation.

"Copy that, you know what to do now," the voice replied.

"Copy that," he said and closed the call. The call would be untraceable and all he had to do now was ensure no evidence of the attack was ever found.

As soon as he was out over the ocean he operated the aircraft's self-destruct function, something all CDF vehicles were fitted with to ensure no hostile force could ever gain an advantage over them if it was captured. Once the timer was set he ejected from the cock-pit. The 'g' force of the rockets thrusting him out of the cock-pit high into the air was nothing he wasn't used to, all the same it still made his butt clench.

The rockets stopped and his ascent slowed and then the para-chute deployed giving him time to watch the fireworks.

The timer ran down and the aircraft exploded into a million tiny pieces. It was engineered so that the blast tore apart the craft destroying everything in it so that even if any of it was recovered it would be almost impossible to reverse engineer it into a viable aircraft.

As he watched the debris scatter over a massive area over the ocean he saw a small craft bobbing about on the water below.

This was his exfil. In moments he had splash landed in the ocean and released his harness so he wouldn't be dragged down by the weight of the chair. Seeing the small boat he began to swim toward it.

It was difficult swimming in his flight suit but he finally reached the edge of the boat and reached up to the side to get aboard.

There was one person sitting watching him, a cold expression on his lean face and another operating the controls who kept his attention on the instruments.

"Give me a hand, will you?" he said to the man with the dead eyes.

He reached out a hand and the man with the dead eyes moved closer as if to help him. Instead of offering a hand though, his hand held a pistol which he put against the pilot's forehead and fired. The bullet blasted through his skull exiting out the back of his head in a red stream that stained the water behind him for several feet.

The pilot's eyes rolled up inside their sockets as his head was jerked back from the impact. His brain shut down immediately as the pressure wave from the bullet passing through destroying it. Slowly, he released his grip on the side of the boat and sank into the water where his flight suit would drag him down to the bottom. It would be months before his body would be found and by that time, after the fish had feasted on him there would be nothing left to recognise him except his DNA. It would be too late to tie him to any of this and the trail would be cold and as dead as he was.

"Okay, take us back, we're done here," the man with the dead eyes told the driver.

Chapter 78

Mi7 Hq

On their return to headquarters Duncan and his partner went straight to C's office where he was already waiting for them.

"Good work you two," he said as they took the offered seats in front of the desk.

"Thank you, sir," Sanchez replied.

Duncan was still operating in mission mode so he ignored the compliment and instead asked, "Who called in the air assault on them sir?"

C looked at him, his expression never altering, "We're still working on that," he said.

"Are you saying that no one in the CDF ordered that assault, sir?" he asked.

Sanchez looked from C to Duncan, her confusion written all over her face.

"What is going on here, who called that air assault on us? Are you saying you don't know sir?" she asked adding her voice to the conversation.

"That's exactly what I'm saying. No one is taking responsibility for it at the CDF which doesn't make sense because if someone had, they would be celebrating in the rescue of the President looking to bolster their position as the new head of the CDF," C said.

"Then we have a new player in the game then," Duncan said.

C looked at him and slowly nodded his agreement. By his closed off expression, he hadn't wanted to say it for all the connotations it brought to light. It was almost as if him not saying it somehow delayed the inevitability of it being real and therefore something they had to consider, and more importantly, deal with.

"Unfortunately, it does seem that way," he said.

"Hold on, are you saying there was another group, or organisation out there who have the resources to order an aerial assault like that? That would mean they have an incredible infrastructure to get their hands on a jet like that," she said.

"That's exactly what we mean," C agreed.

"Do we know where the jet came from, and who flew it?" Duncan asked.

"It came from Vander Air Base and the pilot was Captain Bill Sykes. Nothing about this makes sense because Sykes was a decorated officer, he'd flown many missions and had an exemplary career so why would he suddenly steal a F75 and attack the President on that roof?" C said.

"Moreover sir, how did he know about it, wasn't it supposed to be top secret. I was told a complete communications blackout was in effect to prevent news of it leaking out, so how did he know where to attack? Duncan asked.

"Another good point," C confirmed, "all we have at this time are questions. We have nothing to go on, no leads and the jet was destroyed over the ocean. We have nothing to work from on that score either."

"What about the pilot, has he been found sir?" Sanchez asked.

"No, he disappeared as well. Whoever planned this did an extremely good job in covering their tracks," C told them.

"What happens now sir?" Duncan asked.

"Well, you two have earned yourselves some R and R, take a couple of weeks off and get some rest. The rest of us will get on with the fallout from the attack by Raine on the President, sorry, former President and his council. I'm sure there will be questions asked once the new government is appointed. Then we have the rebuilding to consider once we've recovered all the bodies from the attack sites. We have some hard work ahead of us and it's going to take some time to recover from all of this."

"In the meantime, we could be vulnerable to attack from anyone out there who fancies their chances now that we have taken this hit," Duncan said, "I'm sure that will also be a priority for the new head of the CDF."

"You let them deal with that problem, you've earned your time off. Go have some fun, get some rest and when you return, I hope we'll have a better handle on this whole situation," C said.

"I certainly could do with a good night's sleep," Sanchez admitted and as she looked at her partner she said, "I think you owe me a dinner, now we're off the clock, you have no more excuses."

Duncan gave her a sideways glance, not quite knowing how to respond to that. He returned his eyes to his boss then said, "If there's nothing else sir?"

"Dismissed, go have some fun," C replied then to Sanchez said, "Go gentle on him."

Sanchez smiled, "I can't guarantee that sir, but I'll make sure he's in one piece when it's time to come back to work," she said.

"I'm right here you know," Duncan said confusion furrowing his brow.

"Come on, let's get out of here before C changes his mind," Sanchez said, "we can decide where to go for our dinner on our way out."

"Don't I get a say in any of this?" he asked as they got to their feet.

C said, "It doesn't seem so. If I were you, I'd just go with it. Who knows, you might even have some fun." As the two of them left the office he had to smile. Sanchez seemed determined to get through his barrier and make human contact with him. Who knows, it might make him a better person. Ever since he'd known Pryde he had never known him have any close friends, he seemed almost incapable of making that connection. Some people found his aloofness a problem. Now here was a woman who seemed able to cope with it and who wanted to spend time with him.

It would be interesting to see how this develops.

Putting that thought aside, he returned to the mountain of work he had in front of him, slightly jealous of the two of them that they had time off to relax. Not for him though, this was the burden of command and because of that he had given his life to his work. In that respect Duncan and he had something in common, Duncan had few friends because of his inability to connect, his was a choice of putting his job before anything else.

He turned on his monitor and returned to his work.

Epilogue

The long room was brightly lit as everyone took their place at the long table.

There were no names used here and all the participants used face coverings and voice distortion so that no one knew the identity of any of the people present. Everyone had a number and at the head of the table sat Number One.

"Let us bring this emergency meeting to order," the person at the head of the table said. All Faces turned to look toward them.

"Colonel Hausner acted without approval and forced us to act against him," Number One said.

He continued, "Because of his actions we had to take extreme measures to cover any connection with this group and therefore he has cost us another member. This is not important though, what is important is the disconcerting aspect of the break in discipline. For one of our order to make a decision like this, acting on his own, is beyond belief and will not go unpunished. The order has been given to sanction his entire family. A beach of this nature will not ever be tolerated and this message is being sent to all our members throughout the galaxy. Should anyone consider doing the same, these are the consequences they will face."

Quiet surrounded them as they listened to the altered voice. If fear was present, it was kept well hidden behind all the face coverings but by the silence alone Number One knew they had heard and had understood.

There was a zero-tolerance policy governing this secretive group, any disturbance, any break of protocol was met by the only penalty they had, death. Not just their death though, should any rule be broken the rule breaker was terminated along with every member of their family so that everyone involved knew that the consequences of their actions reached far and wide.

Not once in several decades had this rule been invoked so it was clear that certain members had grown complacent, this would let them know it was a rule still to be feared and followed implicitly.

"While we are here, there was an attack on our Dust plant on Praxis that saw it destroyed. Our supply from this facility has been severely curtailed and we are losing money because of it. Where are we on learning who was behind the destruction of our manufacturing facility?" Number One asked.

Someone half way down the table began to speak, "We still have not learned who the individual was Number One. He seemed to evade all our scanners and sensors. It appears he was wearing a camouflage suit that kept his identity hidden. None of our operatives who challenged him have given a reliable description of the perpetrator except to say he was extremely capable. It is our belief he was an operative of some agency, not just because of his training but his method of ingress and egress to and from the facility. He had resources that rival our own. In short he left no trace."

"Reach out to all our members in every intelligence service, every military Special Forces group and learn the identity of this person. Find him and kill him." Number One said coldly. "Number Four, I am putting you in charge of this operation. I want it handled personally, and there no errors, understood?" he concluded.

At that point Number Four put a hand to his earbud as a call came in. He listened for a short while then held up his hand wanting Number One's attention.

"Sir, I have just received some information that pertains to our present discussion," he said when the leader looked his way.

"Go ahead," he replied.

"I have had a team working around the clock trying to ascertain this operative's name and they have come up with one."

"Don't make me ask Number Four," One said.

"The agent who attacked our facility on Praxis works for the Ministry of Intelligence. His name is Commander Duncan Pryde."

It was impossible to perceive what impression learning this name had on the leader due to the face covering, but Number Four suspected he was pleased.

Finally, after savouring the deliciousness of having a target to aim at, he could now use the entire resources of his group to bring this person to task for meddling in affairs that were none of his concern. He said, "Find him, and kill him."

Unknown to Duncan he now had a target painted on his back, one that would bring the might of an organisation he had no idea existed down on him. Things were about to become very interesting for him.

Very soon indeed.

The end,
for now.

Acknowledgments

I would like to thank everyone who helped me with this book, my partner Joyce Johnson for her invaluable insight into character development and her undying support. Also, I would like to thank all the staff at Red Penguin Books for their support and belief in me, from the editorial staff to the cover art designers and of course, the Head Penguin herself, Stephanie Larkin. You all have my love and thanks.

Also by Jan Domagala